SPEAR HAVOC

SPEAR HAVOC

ALTERNATIVE HISTORIES

C. R. MAY

September 2019

COPYRIGHT

This collection of short stories is a work of fiction. The names, characters and incidents portrayed in it, while at times based on real figures, are purely the work of the author's imagination.

ISBN 978-1-9996695-2-2

Spear Havoc is dedicated to the unnamed uncle of Abbot Æthelwig of Evesham who '...died in Harold's war against the Norse.'

GLOSSARY

Burh - A network of fortified towns in Anglo-Saxon England built primarily as local military strongpoints. They also had a secondary role in providing a safe haven for the surrounding communities in time of war in which trade and the minting of coins could carry on in relative safety.

Butsecarl - Sailor-Warrior - a shipborne fighter.

Chevalier - A knight.

Churl - A commoner in Anglo-Saxon society - the lowest class of free man.

Destrier - A warhorse.

Dragon - A generic name for the many classes of warship. A longship.

Earl/Jarl - A regional lord responsible for administrating a province on behalf of the king for whom he collected taxes, duties and owed military service.

Fyrd - The local militia of Anglo-Saxon England, in which all free men were obliged by law to either serve when called upon or contribute toward its upkeep.

Gonfalon - A type of heraldic banner, often carried into battle.

Housecarl - House-man. A bodyguard or retainer to a powerful earl/jarl or king.

Hundred - A land division within English shires for military and judicial purposes.

Sokemen - A term used in the old lands of the Danelaw to describe those under the sway of another - tenants.

Thegn - A minor nobleman in Anglo-Saxon England.

Wapentake - Weapon-take - the counterpart in the old areas of the Danelaw of the southern English Hundred.

1

BLOOD PRICE

The Kattegat - 9 August 1062

Finn Arnason gripped the backstay, placing a foot on a wale polished by countless booted feet. He hailed the king across the waves. 'It's growing late, lord,' he said with an instinctive glance to the West. The sun was a balefire, the horizon aflame. 'The nights are short at this time of the year, maybe we should wait until morning?' Sweyn Estridsson, king of Danes cupped a hand to his mouth, calling a reply to his underling as the sleek longships churned the surface of the sea all around them. 'We have Hardrada outnumbered and trapped with his back to the shore Finn,' he said with a triumphant grin. 'We may never have a better chance to rid ourselves of the tyrant. Press on: enact our plan and the day will be ours, your brother avenged.'

The Norwegian's eyes swept the sea, taking in the mighty fleet porpoising north as the king turned away. Three hundred ships in battle array was a sight to warm the heart of any fighting man, and God knew that he had seen enough of that over the years, first as a loyal follower of the man he now hoped to see dead before the coming battle ended and latterly as a jarl of Danes. Finn reflected on the cause of his defection to the southern kingdom as his gaze moved inboard to encompass the men of his war band. The lads were rechecking straps, gobbets of spit spattering steel as sharpening stones were swept the length of blades long since honed to a razor-like edge. He let out a snort: devils every one of them; battle hardened killers. Eleven summers had passed since Hardrada had knowingly sent Finn's brother Kalf to his death in a raid on the Danish Island of Funen. King Sweyn was right, the day had arrived to rid the world of the Norwegian despot.

The harsh cry of a lookout broke into his thoughts, and Finn raised his chin to peer beyond the stem post as men gave their blades a final sweep for luck and returned them to their scabbards. A flash of light from a mast top weathervane, glimpsed rather than seen in the swell; but the following wave lifted the ship, and the jarl watched as the striped sail of an enemy dragon came into full view.

The helmsman sniffed at his side. 'They have seen us too, look at her fly.' The grizzled veteran threw his lord a wry look. 'That sail is as taut as a bishop's cassock, we will not catch her.'

Finn snorted as he made a rejoinder. 'The guard ship might report our arrival, but Hardrada will stay and fight despite our numbers. He may be a bastard, but he is no coward.'

The final headland was receding astern as the crews of the Danish fleet worked the braces, angling the yards to hunt the wind, and as the wide bay opened up the helmsmen put the steering oar hard over to come about at the end of the final dogleg. With the westerly now blowing directly over the stern the ships bounded forward, and as the nearness to danger increased with every moment Finn's housecarls moved aft to support their lord. Thorvald Helgison offered up the *brynja* as he came; Finn ducked inside, straightening like a diver breaking the surface as the mail shirt unrolled down his body with a metallic swish. Egil Jarlaskald was there, the jarl-poet all toothy grin and freckles, and Finn responded with a grin of his own as he fastened his helm and took up his bow.

The enemy longship was a league ahead, and despite the need to remain in formation the Danish fleet was clearly gaining with every passing moment. Within a short while the Norwegian ship shortened sail, and oars sprouted from the flanks as it attempted to steer a direct course for the head of the bay. Finn's helmsman turned his face landward as he sought out the cause, uttering a curse as it revealed itself to his practised eye. 'The trees are acting as a wind break,' he growled before spitting over the side in disgust. 'We shall all be rowing soon.'

Finn barely heard as he craned his neck to peer past the place where the frantic rowing of the enemy crewmen was beating the surface to foam, and excitement gripped him as he saw the confirmation that king Sweyn's plan had worked. Go-betweens had agreed the location and day for the battle which was intended to decide the war between the two kings, a conflict which had already lasted more than a dozen years. Each year Hardrada would scathe the coastal regions of the Danish kingdom, but with the ending of the campaigning season Sweyn would return to reclaim his land. Even the sack of Hedeby, the great trading centre at the head of Slienfjord had failed to shift the allegiance of the Danish folk from their natural lord. The mouth of the River Nisâ in Finn's own jarldom of Halland had been agreed as the place where the issue would be decided once and for all, but the wily king of Danes had lingered in the South until the day had passed.

Thinking the enemy had cried off King Harald had sent the levy men, the *bondaherrin*, home as he prepared to lead his choice troops on their annual harrying of Danish lands. Spy ships watched them go, flying south to bring the news to Sweyn as soon as the Norwegians were over the horizon. King Harald's fleet was now in full view, despite the waning light; outthought and outnumbered two to one, Hardrada must fall.

In the lee of the land now Finn watched the sail of his own ship slacken as the wind spilled from it, and as oars slid from ports to stroke the sea all around he watched with satisfaction as the helmsmen of the Halland ships began to guide their charges to the rear of the fleet.

A mile ahead Hardrada's ships were coming together to form the fighting platform which would utilise their strengths. Built to journey the spume filled wastes of the northern ocean, the bows of the Norwegian dragon ships would tower above the Danish hulls which were more suited for use in the shallower seas and estuaries of the South. Roped together they would form a formidable barrier against the attackers, but the predictability of the action had allowed Sweyn and his leaders to devise a plan which should overcome the manoeuvre. Finn Arnason was also a Norwegian as were the majority in his flotilla, and they sailed the same northern built dragons as the countrymen whom fate had made their enemy. Placed as a reserve when the armies came together, it was planned that they would overwhelm Hardrada's defences at a crucial point in the battle.

Heavily outnumbered the Norwegians had anchored the flanks of the line to the shallows at either side of the River Niså — had it not been the fact that it was exactly what the Danes had expected the defence would have been insurmountable. Fearful of fire arrows, Finn watched as the Danish dragons stowed their sails and the first darts began to cloud the air. As the attacking force they would normally have been forced to row until they could grapple the enemy ships, losing men along the way. But the presence of Finn's ships to the rear had allowed Sweyn's fleet to form their own platform early, as the ships of the reserve moved in to nudge them onward.

They were within range now, and Finn flashed a smile as he nocked the first arrow. 'Time to join the fray, I think!' Thorvald and Egil moved in to his flanks as Finn stretched the bowstring for the first time that evening, standing four-square as their shields were raised to protect their lord, and the first dart left the bow as battle horns blared and the clamour of war filled the sultry air. It was the signal for the men in Finn's fleet to add their own bolts to the deadly arrow storm, and as the deck shuddered beneath his feet and the jarl knew that the two fleets had come together, Egil Jarlaskald spoke a verse:

Halland's jarl was bending his bow throughout
the fight,
Raining a shower of arrows on the red shields
of Norway,
As bloody spear-points opened holes in iron
armour;
Shields were pierced by arrows from Finn's
deadly dragon.

The signal came that the two fleets had grappled, and Finn watched as crewmen lashed stout ropes to the stern of the Danish ships in front and another arrow sped away into the dusk. The oarsmen had their eyes fixed upon him, each rower protected by a man with a shield as they awaited the command to pull, and Finn lowered his bow momentarily as his eyes moved out to scan the ships to ether side. The men in the bows were raising an arm, the ties were secure, and as the sky bled crimson Finn Arnason, Jarl of Halland, gave the order to row the fleets into deeper water.

THORVALD HELGISON PLUCKED at his sleeve, and Finn recognised the relief in his words as he spoke. 'A boat!' The jarl tore his gaze away from the fighting and looked. A little *skipsbåt*, the smaller ship's boats which many of the larger dragons carried for messaging and inshore work was heading towards them, the man in the bow careful to hold the white shield of Denmark aloft to reassure the men in the reserve of their allegiance.

Finn turned back to follow the fighting, puffed up with pride at the valiant defence offered by his countrymen despite his enmity towards their king. Brands cast a spectral glow over the carnage on board the Norwegian ships as men stabbed and slashed in the gloom. Sword and axe blades flamed before they were swallowed again by the night, here and there a face appeared from the heaving mass, blood-red in the firelight, only to be snuffed out in an instant. It was a vision of Hell, but the jarl was no stranger to the push of shields and he ached to join the fray.

The small rowboat bumped against the strakes of his own ship, and willing hands hauled the leading man aboard as his companions stroked oars to keep their station against the ebbing tide. Crewmen pointed his way, and the Dane hurried aft brandishing king Sweyn's tokens before him as he confirmed the source of the message he carried. Finn nodded that he speak even before he had drawn up before him.

'I come directly from King Sweyn, lord,' the messenger

announced. 'The king says that the enemy flanks are fully exposed, and the time to take Blood Price for the death of your brother has arrived.'

Finn suppressed a snort as all eyes on the ship looked his way. The communication was cunningly worded. Sweyn was aware that he was expecting Norwegians to fight against fellow countrymen, victory may very well depend upon it, so a gentle reminder of the reason why they were there would be far more effective than an outright order. He nodded as he tossed his bow gratefully aside, flexing fingers made sore and numb by the repeated plucking of the bowstring. 'How goes the fight?'

The Dane's face lit up. 'The fight goes well, lord,' he chirruped proudly. 'The king's housecarls hold the enemy bows and the grapples remain firmly in place.'

Finn's eyes flashed. 'Then it is time to send this *Harðráði* to Hell. God keeps no place for Hard-rulers in Heaven, nor those who knowingly send loyal men on an errand of death.' Egil Jarlaskald was his banner man, and the jarl indicated that he signal the attack with a curt nod. The battle horn came up, and Egil spat to clear his mouth an instant before the familiar *yip-yip-yip* filled the darkness. The signal was taken up on the other ships, and as the oarsmen began to pull towards the enemy wings, now left fearfully exposed far from the safety of the shallows by the pull of Danish oars and the outgoing tide, Finn led his housecarls to the bow. Thorvald was prow man, the very tip of the *svinfylking*, and the prow beast soon disappeared behind his huge frame as the other members of Finn's bodyguard formed a protective wedge about their lord to complete the swine array. As banner man Egil took up position to his lord's rear, and as the wooden wall of the first ship in the Norwegian fleet began to grow in his vision and the war banner unfurled in the breeze, Finn thrilled to the words as Egil spoke again:

> *Battle-eager Finn bade his crew be steadfast,*
> *warriors made a bulwark along the wales.*
> *The doughty jarl of Halland lined his dragon*
> *ship with a wall of living shields;*
> *No foe could find a gap there.*

A faint lightening in the sky to the East told of the approaching day, and Finn realised with a start that the fighting had lasted throughout the hours of darkness. Faces began to appear on the enemy ship, pale and drawn after the rigours of the night, but a volley of javelins drove them back and the jarl hefted his shield as he tightened the grip on his sword and prepared to board. A quick look to starboard confirmed that the ships in his formation were alongside, the furthermost already pulling ahead to sweep around the rear of the enemy battle-raft, and his war cry was taken up all along the line as the hulls finally crashed together:

Onward! Onward! Freemen!

Arrows hissed overhead to mottle enemy shields as Norwegian men rushed back to repulse the attack. Thorvald scythed his war axe in a death dealing arc, and with an animal cry he was over the bows to disappear from sight as he crashed into his opponents, the first man to board the enemy vessel as his reputation demanded. As the wolf light of the predawn grew, his housecarls were vaulting the gap as they came to their friend's aid; Finn followed on, landing on a deck made slick by blood as his men chased the opposition away.

With the return of daylight the jarl was able to gauge the depth the Norwegian defences for the first time: the enemy fleet had been arrayed in three ranks, fifty ships to a line, each roped to its neighbours by a web of running rigging, hawsers and spars. Masts had been set athwart the beam forming a series of barricades between the defenders and king Sweyn's Danes. But despite their hard work the ramparts and bulwarks now acted against the defenders, segmenting the ships and making a cohesive defence all but impossible now that the danger came from the southern flank. Finn gave a grudging nod of recognition to his countrymen's efforts to turn a disparate collection of ships into an impregnable fortress, despite the fact that his attack had now rendered their efforts worse than useless as the last of the enemy crewmen on the captured ship were finished off near the stern. The look had shown him the location of the prize which would draw every man of reputation in the fleet like drunks to a skirt. In the very centre of the formation Harald Hardrada's *Landøyðan*, the Land-waster battle flag famous throughout the north, flew above the longship of the king. Egil had seen it too, and he leaned in to speak as men continued to teem aboard and those already on deck regrouped to renew the attack. 'It's a strong position, lord,' he said grudgingly. 'And he has Hakon Ivarsson and his Tronds alongside.'

Finn shrugged. 'None said it would be easy, the men of Trondheim never did shrink from a fight. But the Danes have all but cleared the first row of ships — once their flags are seen aboard the king's dragon it should go quickly as the rest lose heart.'

Under attack now from three directions, the men on the ships immediately before him were beginning to show the first signs that they thought the day, barely birthed, was already lost. Allied to his own attack, the threat of encirclement was now very real as the outflanking Hallanders to the east began to pour volleys of spears and arrows onto the rear of the defenders, and Finn watched gleefully as the rearmost of king Harald's ships began to hack through the ropes which bound them together and prepared to flee.

The captured dragon was filled with his men now, with more crowding the bows of his own ships as they too sought to carry shield and spear against the foe. The attack had to be followed up quickly and the jarl filled his lungs, raising his sword to the brightening sky as he bellowed the words which would unleash them again:

Onward! Onward! Freemen!

The battle cry was the sign for those following on to unleash a barrage of spears at the defenders. The darts flashed overhead in a blur of movement to bury themselves in the opposing shields with a hollow *thunk*, and the moment he knew that the last had been released Finn was leading the charge across the deck. The volley had caused havoc among those lining the side of the next longship in the defence, and the jarl saw the panic and indecision in the eyes of Hardrada's men as they wrestled with the conflicting needs to remove the spears from their shield faces and brace the great board to receive the attack. In truth they had no time to act before the leading attackers were upon them, and all along the line men were stomping on spear shafts to open up the defenders. As the boards were dragged forward and down by the action, others were already moving in to stab and thrust at the now exposed faces and upper bodies of the defenders. Thorvald Helgison was just ahead of his lord, and as the blade of his war axe came down Finn made ready to strike. The beard of the axe hooked a shield rim, and as the board was tugged down and away Finn's sword flashed to transfix its first victim that day. Before the man could fall Finn was leaping the wales, crashing to the enemy deck as his sword continued to hack to left and right. A spear point hardened from the scrum and he made to duck, but the haft of an axe came up to knock the blade up and away before it could pierce his neck and Finn knew that Thorvald was back at his side.

As the rest of his guardsmen leapt aboard to widen the breach, Finn snatched a quick look along the line. The enemy shield fort had been pierced in several places, and the defenders were moving back to back in their desperation to survive the onslaught. Already the next wave of attackers were channelling through as they kept up the momentum of the attack they called the Snow-slip. All men of Norway had witnessed such a thing on the steep sided slopes of home; starting off as barely a ripple in the snow cover high on the mountainside, the fall quickly gathered strength as it moved downhill until very soon it became a roaring wave which swept all before it. By leapfrogging forward even before the first enemy deck had been cleared of foemen, Finn's assault quickly developed into such an unstoppable force. Men who thought themselves safe in the rear only moments before found to their surprise and consternation that the enemy were already upon them, and as the attack snowballed resistance to it grew increasingly ragged until it collapsed completely.

The familiar sound of spearpoints thudding into shield faces dragged Finn's attention back to the front, and as the jarl watched the wide boards were dragged down and sword and spear blades danced again. In moments the second wave were over the side, forcing their way aboard the next longship in the fighting platform as they drove the attack forward. Finn opened his mouth to call his fighters together, but a glance told him that the struggle here was already over and the men were set to go. The jarl's sword jabbed the air again, but the exiles did not wait for his lead as the war cry came again and they set off across the deck.

Men were still locked in death-duels as Finn and his

crewmen came over the side, but they were ignored as the fighters pushed their way past and fixed their eyes on the next ship in line. Already Finn could see that the Snow-slip was working as the number of enemy shields facing them began to lessen with every deck cleared, and he spied a breach as the javelins hissed overhead once again and led his men towards it. Again his sword came down as he leapt the gap between the ships, the blade lopping off the top of a skull before his victim had time to raise his shield to ward off the blow, but there was no time to watch the man fall as a flash of movement caused him to drag his own shield upwards. Faster than a heartbeat the *crack* of splintering wood filled his ears as a powerful strike knocked him sideways, and although stunned by the force of the blow years of experience caused the jarl to throw his shoulder into the back of the board as he sought to close with his attacker. With the side of his face now flattened against the back of the shield Finn felt a kick of relief as he saw the toe of an axe blade little more than an inch before his nose, and he twisted the board to trap it there as his feet scrabbled for purchase on the wallowing deck. He could sense the desperation of his attacker through the boards of his shield as the man worked to free the weapon, but Finn's sword was already coming up, sawing back and forth as he worked the blade around the rim to stab where his face should be. An agonised roar cut the air the moment the enemy blade came free, and Finn took a backward pace as his housecarls flowed around him. Thorvald, his axe blade dripping with gore bustled to his side, and the reason for the unexpected disappearance of his opponent became obvious the moment that Finn glanced down, the fist still gripping the axe and the shattered stump of a forearm all that remained in sight of his assailant.

As the last defenders were driven back and javelins were

raised to open the assault on the next ship in line, the jarl grabbed the opportunity to raise his head and look beyond it. His eyes widened as he did so, and he came to realise just how close the headlong rush had carried them in such a short time. There, three hulls distant, lay the prize that everyman in the fleet was fighting towards, the longship containing king Harald gleaming like a newly hammered nail in the soft August light canting from the East. Constructed the previous winter on the strand up at Nidaros, the *Ormen* was a giant of thirty-five oar benches — seventy rowers all-found. As befitted her name the prow was surmounted by a gilded dragon head above a gilt bow, the golden sides streaked red with the blood of axe and spearmen telling the tale of the desperate fighting which had taken place that night. Upriver the ship's stern curled into an enormous dragon tail, and beneath it Finn saw the bear-like figure of the Norwegian king for the first time in a year or more beneath Land-waster, the hated raven war flag of Oðinn, the false god of their ancestors.

Egil spoke, echoing Finn's fears as they watched the fighting reach its climax. 'King Sweyn is aboard the *Ormen* lord,' he said sadly. 'It looks as if we will have to content ourselves with witnessing the tyrant's fall from afar.' Finn looked and knew in his heart that his banner man spoke truthfully. The war flag of king Sweyn was already amidships, every foot of decking between the dragon headed prow and the mast fish crammed with the white shields of Denmark. He was about to reply when Egil spoke again, the shock in his voice profound. 'Jarl Hakon has men cutting the ropes binding him to the *Ormen*!' As Finn switched his gaze to the steering platform of the Trondheim ship, Thorvald Helgison voiced his disgust. 'Hakon Ivarsson abandoning his lord at the time of greatest need.' The huge housecarl spat. 'What more can you expect of Tronds?'

Finn was about to say his piece when he saw the reason for the assumed betrayal. 'No,' he said as an arm came up to point. 'He has taken young Olaf Haraldsson on board, he means to save the boy.'

The trio looked on as the ship finally managed to break free from the ropes which bound her to the king's dragon and began to pull upstream. As the northern ship moved away Finn spoke again: 'Egil?'

'Yes, lord?'

'Sound the horn to end the fighting. We cannot reach the *Ormen* now that the jarl's ship has removed the bridge: we are killing fellow Norwegians for no gain.'

As the falling note filled the air and the two sides backed away, both sets of fighting men turned their heads to the North, awestruck that they must soon bear witness to the death of the man who had always seemed indestructible. The Danes were closing in as more and more of king Sweyn's housecarls swarmed aboard the *Ormen* and fought their way aft. The ship on the far side of Hardrada's had already been cleared of Norwegian defenders, and a knot of Danish bowmen were gathered at the stern loosing shaft after shaft at the outflanked king's guard. With a final surge the *Landøyðan* went down, blades flashed in the morning light, and hoarse cries of victory mixed with the lamentations of defeat as they saw the king was dead.

Finn's mind wandered back over the years as a wistful mood gripped them all, and his gaze drifted across to the slight figure of the king's son as jarl Hakon's ship burst through the final Danish defences and pulled for deeper water. As a younger man Finn had followed Harald's half-brother Olaf into exile among the Rus: returning together they had fought to reclaim his throne in battle at a place called Stiklestad. Olaf had been killed, but young Harald Sigurdsson had fought alongside them and got away with his life. That Harald's treachery had made them enemies he regretted, but the blood feud was over, the tyrant dead, and peace could return to a northern kingdom now set to be ruled by a twelve year old lad.

AFTERWORD

Most who have any knowledge of the events leading up to the battles in 1066, know that Harald Hardrada made his reputation and fortune in the service of the rulers in Constantinople. However few realise that he returned from the South fully twenty years before he finally met his death fighting against Harold Godwinson's army outside York. These were years of constant warfare as Harald sought to bring the Danish kingdom under Norwegian rule following the collapse of Cnut the Great's empire, which had included not only Denmark and Norway but England too. All the main protagonists in the above story were well known to one another, sometime friends and allies; not only had the kings Harald and Sweyn campaigned together against the previous king Magnus the Good, an illegitimate son of Harald's half-brother Olaf, they were in fact uncle and nephew. It would take a full size book to tell the story of those years and this is not the place, but suffice to say that Harald Sigurdsson earned the nickname Hardrada, Hard-ruler, during this period of his life by being the meanest snake in a nest of adders.

The battle at the River Niså happened largely as told in

the tale above. It seems that the date and time had been arranged between the two kings for a final showdown, and that either by accident or design the Danes arrived late. Harald had by then sent home the half of his fleet composed of the *bondaherrin* of the regional levy, retaining only his senior men and full time warriors as he prepared to harry king Sweyn's kingdom as he had practically every summer for almost two decades. Outnumbered two to one and trapped in the bay, Harald roped his ships together and waited for the Danes to attack. In the real battle Harald either stationed his second in command Hakon Ivarsson of Trondheim on the southern wing of the formation or held him in reserve, while king Sweyn kept his own second, Finn Arnason, close by in the centre of the battle line, perhaps to ensure the loyalty of the Norwegian exile who was not only married to Hardrada's niece but a one time staunch supporter of the king. They fought throughout the night, but as daybreak approached and the Norwegians began to give way, a boat was sent to Hakon ordering him to launch his attack. The Norwegian ships were generally larger and their occupants seasoned veterans, and when they came upon the weaker Danish ships they quickly rolled up the line. King Sweyn escaped, but Finn Arnason refused to flee and was captured.

By switching the dispositions of the opposing fleets I was able to reverse the result of the battle for my reworking of history. With the Norwegian leaders now concentrated at the centre of the fighting and unable to react to changing circumstances, the superior Danish numbers are decisive. Finn Arnason now leads the outflanking force, moving around to crush the weaker ships on the Norwegian wings. Already outnumbered and having fought through the night, Hardrada's fleet is overwhelmed and the king killed.

In reality the Danes and Norwegians realised that they

had fought each other to a standstill, the two kings concluding an unconditional peace treaty two years later in 1064. By this pact both kings recognised the other as rightful ruler in their respective kingdoms, foregoing any claims to reparations of land or treasure and exchanging prisoners. Without an enemy to fight for the first time since his early teens the warlike Harald Hardrada would become a magnet attracting disaffected nobles looking for heavyweight support to repair their fortunes; within two years Tostig, the ousted earl of Northumbria and brother of the English king Harold Godwinson, duly arrived in Oslo.

In our timeline Harald Sigurdsson's son, the twelve year old Olaf who was present at the battle, becomes king on the death of his father at Niså, just as he did in 1066 after Harald's death in England. With the boy who was to become known to history as Olaf the Peaceable already on the throne in Norway any threat to Northern England is removed, and free from Norwegian raids king Sweyn of Denmark can confidently send even greater numbers of Danish troops to aid his kinsman Harold Godwinson than he did in reality. William of Normandy would have faced not a tired and depleted force at Hastings, but the full might of an English army fighting on home soil, reinforced by large numbers of elite Danish housecarls.

2

THE EXILE

London - April 1057

Edward sighed with contentment and stretched out, wedging a foot to lever off one riding boot after the other. Turning aside he took up a stoup and toasted his friend in the unfamiliar tongue: *'Wæs hæl, biscop!'*

His companion chuckled with delight, before making the customary reply to the English salute with a gleam in his eye: *'Drinc hæl, Éadweard! Heahgeweorc!'*

The pair shared a knowing look, and Edward shook with laughter as the older man translated the latest addition to his slowly increasing vocabulary into Magyar: 'Heahgeweorc! — Excellent!'

Edward Edmundson shook his head in dismay. 'I do not even know my own tongue, bishop.' He took a sip of wine and sighed. 'I would be lost here without your guidance. You have the heartfelt gratitude of myself and my family for accompanying us to our homeland.'

The conversation was cut short as a shadow fell across the pair, and the ætheling glanced up to see that one of their

Hungarian servants was hovering at his side. Edward indicated that she should speak with the flick of a finger.

'Lady Agatha sends her apologies, lord. She asks if Bishop Beneta could spare a few moments to help with the food we have been served.' The ætheling's eyes widened in question and the woman explained. 'The children are reluctant to try most of the dishes….' She hesitated before settling on a reason which she hoped would cause as little offence as possible; in time her master looked set to become the king of this land after all. 'They are unfamiliar with many of the ingredients and the manner in which they have been prepared.'

Edward caught a fleeting look of resignation flash across the face of his friend and pulled a sympathetic smile. As one of the few people in that distant land who was fluent in English, he had been the natural choice to accompany the party when the invitation had arrived from the Confessor's court. His sense of duty had compelled him to make the journey from Rekavar, but at nearly seventy years of age his old bones deserved a rest.

Edward regarded the servant as the bishop prepared to rise. 'Tell my wife that he will be along as soon as he feels refreshed.'

The woman hesitated and pulled a face.

Edward chuckled. 'Not good enough?'

The maid winced and shifted uncomfortably. 'The lady was rather insistent, lord.'

Bishop Beneta pulled a wry smile and began to lever himself out of the chair. Patting the prince on the arm for his efforts, he shuffled off with the grateful looking retainer.

Left alone, the man the English were calling Edward the Exile settled back and sipped chilled wine as the waters of the River Thames flowed by beneath him. From his vantage point he could see the great span of London bridge which linked the city to the burh of Southwark. He had marvelled at its great size as they had crossed into the city from the southern bank only that morning, and had eagerly searched for signs of the desperate fighting which had occurred there during the wars of his father and grandfather. It was a mark of that chaotic time in England that the bridge had been defended that day by spear Danes. Forty-three years previously the English king, his own grandfather Æthelræd, had stormed the crossing as his ally the Norwegian Olaf Haraldsson had attacked the bridge from downriver. The central span had been destroyed in the attack, and Edward smiled as a rhyme he had heard in Kiev celebrating the fighting that day drifted into his mind:

London Bridge is broken down,
Gold is won and bright renown,
Shields resounding,
War Horns sounding,
Hildur shouting in the din.
Arrows singing,
Mail coats ringing,
Oðinn makes our Olaf win!

The wharf which edged the northern shore below him buzzed with activity as ships from across the known world unloaded their exotic cargoes. It was clear why the Vikings had returned again and again to the English motherland; the country was groaning with wealth, he had seen it for himself on the journey here from the coast.

But the affluence and vitality of his people was not the only revelation. He had spent his first night on English soil since he had fled the victorious Cnut as a young boy at the port of Dover. They had marvelled at the cliffs as they approached and even his son Edgar, already giddy with excitement on his first sea trip, had paused from mischief making to gape in wonder at the towering white ramparts of his new homeland. To their great surprise they had been welcomed by cheering crowds, both in the port and at the town of Rochester where they had broken their journey to the capital. The children had looked on with mounting excitement as crowds had gathered to chant *Ironside! Ironside!* outside their lodgings in the town, and he had proudly explained that it was the eke name which his own father, King Edmund, had been given by the people for his doughty fighting qualities.

Edmund Ironside had fought the great Danish army of Cnut to a standstill, before agreeing to partition the country to enable the war weary English people time to recover and win back their land. Betrayed, he had soon been murdered and his young sons spirited abroad by the victorious Dane to share his fate. Edward sighed as he remembered his dead brother. Named after their father, the boys had been inseparable during their years in exile, and Edward thought on the injustice of his older brother's death. Far from home, he had not lived to see the day when he would be recalled and declared heir to the kingdom.

The slightest of coughs sounding at his elbow told him that the servant had returned, but as the woman opened her mouth to speak the ætheling was already raising a hand to cut her short. He knew he was expected, and draining the cup Edward took a final look upriver as he stood to go. The sun lay on the western hills, the evening sky blushed scarlet as the day drew on, and a stillness was beginning to descend on the greasy waters of the river as the boatmen hurried home to families and ale houses. Beyond the great sweep of the

Thames stood the king's hall at Thorney, near to the place where the Confessor was building a great stone minster in the latest Romanesque style. Tomorrow he would finally meet with his cousin and be proclaimed heir to the kingdom of the English. A sudden chill ran through him as he thought of the ancestors who had passed through the king's doors in days gone by. So many ghosts stood at his shoulder here.

His humour returned as he approached the room set aside for dining. The family had already gathered and he could hear one of the girls, Margaret or Christina, cry out in exasperation as she attempted to persuade her young brother to act with the manners expected of a Christian prince.

Edward entered the room and smiled as Beneta rose in welcome. The table had been set with a selection of typical English dishes and he hoped that the bishop's experience extended to such things. The older man had already discovered a liking for the drink known as cider, which he had described as "an excellent remedy for sleeplessness" the ætheling recalled with a snort.

He hailed the venerable churchman as he came into the room: 'Bishop, what do you recommend?'

Bishop Beneta sidled over and guided the ætheling towards the table. 'You will be pleased to learn that they have excellent food here, lord,' he said with the expansive sweep of an arm.

Edward forced down a smile as he admonished the old churchman. 'Not excellent bishop: heahgeweorc!'

Agatha glanced across as the men's laughter filled the room, and Edward was gratified to see the happiness there despite the best efforts of the children to ruin the meal. Beneta reached the table and pointed out a certain dish. 'Now this *is* heahgeweorc, lord,' he said enthusiastically. 'I can vouch for it personally. I am told that the king had it specially prepared to introduce you to a food which is widely eaten by your countrymen, irrespective of rank.'

The Exile crinkled his nose. 'What is it? It looks like cake filled with meat.'

Beneta chuckled with delight. 'That is what I thought at first. Apparently it is known as pie. It is tremendously popular here, and I was told that I must ensure that you eat a healthy portion.'

Edward shrugged, reaching across towards the place where a large slice had already been removed from the otherwise perfect circle of the pie. Cutting a wedge of his own he slid it onto a trencher. 'So what does it taste like, this pie?' Turning back, Edward chuckled as the old bishop belched and pulled a pained expression. 'It can't be that bad, surely old friend?'

Beneta wheezed, reaching out to grip his lord's arm as the pain spasmed again. As the old churchman's face became a rictus, his arm shot out in a final selfless act to send Edward's platter spinning from his hand.

AFTERWORD

Of all the 'what ifs' surrounding the problem of who would succeed the childless Edward the Confessor, perhaps the most often overlooked and tragic is the death of Edward the Exile in 1057. Edward and his older brother Edmund were the sons of Edmund Ironside who was king of England briefly in 1016. Having taken up the fight against the Danes following the death of his father, Æthelræd II *Unræd*, Edmund came close to outright victory before he was betrayed by a leading English noble, Eadric Streona (Eadric the grasper). By the terms of the Treaty of Olney, Edmund and the Danish king Cnut agreed to share the kingdom between them. They became royal brothers and sole heir to each other's English lands. Edmund died, probably murdered on Cnut's orders, within weeks, and Cnut and his allies killed or drove abroad any who might pose a threat to their rule.

Even though such leading Englishmen as Edmund Ironside's brother, the popular Eadwig was murdered out of hand, the Ironside's young boys were now the sons of Cnut's sworn brother by the terms of the treaty and therefore posed a different problem for him. Edmund was approaching his first birthday and Edward was a newborn babe. Even Cnut baulked at the outright murder of what were now the baby sons of his brother. There was however a precedent for such situations in the northern world and the Dane took it. The young æthelings were sent abroad to Cnut's half-brother in Sweden in the expectation that they would be murdered there, but he passed the boys on the royal court in Hungary where his sister was queen. Cnut's assassins soon tracked them down, and they were forced to flee again to the Kievan Rus where they grew to adulthood under the protection of Yarolslav the Wise. There they fell in with another exile Andrew of Hungary, and the English brothers returned to the West to help their new friend gain the Hungarian crown in 1046. Edmund died in Hungary no later than 1053, but Edward was now a warrior of renown with a family which included a young son, Edgar. Both males were direct descendants of the old West Saxon line and were the perfect solution to the situation in England regarding the succession. It seemed obvious now that king Edward would die without issue and the pogroms of Cnut forty years earlier had all but eliminated the family.

Edward was sent for and returned to widespread rejoicing. Arriving at Dover he travelled to London where he was to meet the king and be formally recognised as heir to the English throne, but before the meeting occurred the Exile was dead.

There is no record of how this robust descendant of Cerdic and Alfred met his end, but there is no mention of wounding or illness in the chronicles and it must be assumed to have been the work of a poisoner. What does seem certain is that with the death of Edward the Exile, the bloodbath of 1066 became almost inevitable. The Confessor washed his hands of the succession problem and seemed resigned to the chaos which would follow his death. Following duke William's victory at Hastings the Exile's young son, Edgar ætheling, was acclaimed king but never crowned. Although Edgar rebelled several times against Norman rule over the following decades he could make no impression on a land now dotted with impregnable castles and ruled by the iron fist of the Conqueror. The male line of Cerdic which had ruled over at least the southern areas of England for almost six centuries was all but extinguished, and the Anglo-Saxon age ended.

Who would gain by such an act? The pious King Edward cannot have been to blame, the ætheling's return neatly solved all of his succession problems. William of Normandy is a suspect and there is no doubt that he would have ordered such a thing: other men who were regarded as threats by the duke, within the borders of the duchy and without, had died by poisoning. Norman sources claim that King Edward had promised the throne to William as early as 1051, and there were Normans in positions of power in England in 1057 who could have organised the killing.

The finger of suspicion must also point at the Godwinson clan. There is documentary support that Harold Godwinson was involved in bringing the exile home, with strong evidence that he actually travelled to the continent at this time, perhaps as far as Rome. But was Harold contemplating the throne in 1057, if at all? He was certainly the most powerful of king Edward's earls and was well placed to make a bid for the kingship if, as seemed almost certain by then, the Confessor died without producing a son. What better way to eliminate the last of the legitimate heirs to the throne than to help bring them home from distant Hungary and within the reach of his henchmen?

Another contender must be Harold's brother, Tostig. He

shared many of Harold's qualities but appears to have been far more cunning and ruthless. Crucially he seems to have been the favourite of both King Edward and Queen Eadgyth, his sister. As the second eldest surviving son of Godwin and with the support of the royal couple, Tostig too would have everything to gain by the Exile's quick death. Already earl of Northumbria his rule there had been unpopular and heavy handed. He would even go on to murder the sons of important northern nobles who had answered his summons under safe conduct, so removing Edward the Exile would be entirely in character. His rule was so unpopular that the Northumbrians eventually rose against him.

Perhaps Harold saw a chance to remove another man who might stand between him and Edward's throne when he refused to support his brother against the rebels, turning him into the implacable enemy who would fight alongside Harald of Norway in 1066?

The true reason for Edward the Exile's death will never be known, he could even have choked on a slice of pie. Accidents can and do happen.

3

HACON

The duke paced the boggy ground, casting a look of disgust at the angry sky. Yet another blanket of greyness was rolling in from the West, and he hissed a curse before turning back to the armoured group. 'We have to attack,' he spat, 'and soon. If this accursed weather grows any wetter we shall all be growing gills!'

The knights laughed dutifully at their leader's quip, but the truth was they were fast running out of time. As a count in his own right with a good claim to the English throne, Eustace of Boulogne clearly felt himself the equal of the Norman leader, and he made a suggestion as the others averted their eyes. 'Maybe we should withdraw to our encampment?' Eustace threw a look skywards. 'We have perhaps another hour or so of what passes for daylight in this accursed land. If our best fighters act as a rearguard, we still have time to rest and regroup and renew the attack on the morrow.'

Duke William spun on a heel and glared. Not for the first time that day he regretted having the man in his army, and although he had added a healthy number of men to the invading host the count was as trustworthy as a snake. 'And what if the English are arrayed along the ridge line not just to deny us access to the interior,' he spat, 'but corralling us like oxen for the slaughter while the rest of their army makes its way to the battlefield? Have you thought of that?' The duke shook his head. 'No, we attack again. I shall lead the *chevaliers* directly up the roadway and punch through to the usurper. The moment he falls the day is ours.' A murmur of agreement met his announcement and William paused, his eyes shooting daggers at the group. The men were tired out, he knew that, but the cry had been a mere shadow of the throaty roar which had proceeded the first attack at the beginning of the day, and the truth was that a feeling of hopelessness was beginning to chivvy away at even his unshakable faith.

Eustace tried again, and the duke clenched his teeth in frustration as a quick look at the faces in the group showed that the idea had been well received by some. 'If we attack once more, it will be dark by the time we know if we have been successful in breaking through. If thrown back again — we will be trapped in this bog for the rest of the night, within easy reach of English spears.' Eustace glanced to either side as he looked for support. The pause had been expertly judged — just long enough to suggest that that was the likeliest outcome, but not so dragged out to be seen as a clear challenge to the duke's authority. His point made, the count spoke again as William seethed. 'What if the usurper and his horde decide to attack us in our sleep?' Eustace went to continue, but the duke's anger finally boiled over. 'Then at least we should have got them down from that bloody ridge!' William clicked his fingers, pointing angrily to the space where he expected his horse to be. The pageboy blanched, his eyes fixed firmly on the muddy soil of England as he led the animal across. As the duke hauled himself back into the saddle, he cursed beneath his breath. He had known the majority of the men below him for the best part of his life, indeed he owed his life to more than a few of them and he regretted his outburst. He pulled a weary smile as his self control reasserted itself: they were not alone in feeling the strain. 'It's been a hard day,' he said. 'But I should not have wished to spend it in any other company than the men I see before me now. We have come a long way together my friends, let us finish what we started.' Turning away William reached inside his mail shirt, closing his eyes in silent prayer as his lips met the sliver of the True Cross. The relic had been a gift to him from the Pope in Rome, along with the papal banner which now flew, bedraggled and grimy, at his side.

Lord God. Grant me this victory, and I will honour you with a thousand new churches and a hundred monasteries throughout my realm of England.

He forced himself to tuck the pendant away. His action had begun to tread the fine line between devotion and desperation, and he shifted in the saddle as he swept the upturned faces with his gaze. Forcing the mood down deep, he grinned encouragement at them and drew his sword. He had dragged them this far by the sheer force of his will, he could get them to the top of the final hill.

'Tell the trumpeters to signal the general advance: archers; everything. Let us finally breach this "shield wall" and claim that which my cousin, the pious and holy Confessor, promised to me.'

Duke William walked his *destrier* to the base of the slope and looked beyond the bright wall of muscle, steel and leather which lined the crest of the ridge to the graphite grey clouds beyond. A faint lightening away to the West told him that the short October day was almost spent, it would have to be this time or he would lose everything. As his most trusted men mounted and pushed their horses to his side, his mind wandered back over the events of that fateful year.

It had been a year of heady highs and desperate lows. Before the first month had passed he had received the bitter-sweet news from England. King Edward had died childless, but the throne had been usurped by the earl of Wessex, Harold Godwinson. Only two years before Harold had promised him on holy relics that he would support the duke's claim to the throne, a fact that he now conveniently denied. William snorted in a rare display of humour that grim day, guiding the head of his horse westwards as he did so. He knew for certain that Harold lied — he had ordered the relics hidden beneath the cloth himself.

He had browbeaten the faint hearts who said that it could not be done and assembled a vast invasion army. Hundreds of ships had taken shape along the banks of the River Dives. Emissaries had caressed the Pope's ego with their silken tongues and persuaded the pontiff that his was a just cause. He would replace Stigand, the excommunicate archbishop of Canterbury, and order a great reformation of the English church, increasing both its wealth and power.

God Himself had shown his support for the great under-taking, sending Harold's own brother Tostig to raid the coast of the kingdom, and the thrashings of the wounded giant had brought every knight in northern France flocking to his banner like crows to a corpse. And then, just as the army was set, the provisions laid in and ready to sail, the invasion had ground to a halt. Contrary winds had pinned them within the great bay of the River Somme at St Valery, and he had prayed for guidance daily as the summer drew on and the supplies dwindled. Some men said that God had ruled against his invasion — the cowardly began to slink away in the night. But the

Lord had not forsaken him. The same wind which had delayed his own attack until the English had abandoned their coastal watch, had swept the Norwegian army of King Harald Sigurdsson south. Having drawn the usurper's attention the Almighty had backed the wind and William had sailed. Disembarking on the deserted coast he had discovered that Harold was away in the North. Soon news had reached them that the English had won a great victory against the grizzled Viking, but he knew from bitter experience that it would have come at a cost. Harold's army would be exhausted and depleted — so he had laid waste the southern district, Harold's ancestral land, while his enemy raced back south. He was certain that the English would take the bait, and when they moved he would be ready: he would crush them as he had his previous enemies.

Drumbeats and the strident blare of horns broke into his thoughts, and William looked past the knot of knights surrounding him to the foot soldiers beyond as they moved forward and dressed themselves in their battles. The archers were already at the foot of the hill, loosing shafts which vanished into the gloom almost the moment that they left the bowstring. All eyes were turned towards him as they awaited his signal to begin what must be the final advance of the day, and William felt the power of command surge through him again. It was, he realised, the same thrill which had driven Caesar, Alexander and Hannibal on to greatness when all seemed lost.

William savoured the moment as he raised his sword, steadily, deliberately, and the drumming and bugling petered away. He was certain that he stood on the very cusp of greatness and although the English, animated and mocking in their battle line were a distant interruption, the silence of the valley floor was heavy and pregnant with expectation as every man in the army tensed. William's arm stilled for a heartbeat and then the long blade chopped down. As he put back his spurs and his mount gathered speed, the Norman army let out a great roar and surged forward.

HACON PLACED the bloodied axe blade against the curve of his instep and rested the great haft against his waist. Reaching out he took the bowl with a smile, before lowering his head to savour the aroma. 'Ah, pease pudding, my favourite!'

The king's voice carried across from his position at the head of the roadway and a rumble of laughter rolled along the shield wall. 'Hacon, every type of food is your favourite. You would think the Bastard never fed you while you were his captive.'

Despite being well intended his uncle's jibe had drawn the humour from the moment, and Hacon set his face into a frown as he called out for all to hear. 'I, Hacon Sweynson, hereby pledge to make this duke a captive of your own, lord. That you may ransom him dead or alive for our kinsman, my dear cousin Wulfnoth.'

The smile fell from the king's face as he too recalled his youngest brother, held against his will in Normandy these past fourteen years, and the pair — king and nephew — exchanged a look of determination across a field of helmeted heads. But Hacon's words had thrilled those within earshot, and they let their feelings known as the hillside shook once again to a noise like rolling thunder, spear shafts clashing on shield rims as men called their challenges for the hundredth time that day to the invaders massing at the foot of the slope.

He had been barely five years old when other Normans had spirited him away to the duchy, and his memories of that time were hazy. But if he only dimly recalled the flight, and indeed the face of his own father Sweyn — the eldest of earl Godwin's sons who had died the same year — he knew how much he owed the boy who had been snatched alongside him. Wulfnoth Godwinson had been twelve at the time of their abduction, and it was a truism that during the years which followed he had become as a father to him. Harold had brought a great ransom in an effort to retrieve them two years hence, when old king Edward still lived and his uncle was still an earl, but although Hacon had been released the wily duke had insisted that Wulfnoth remain. Now, after what felt like a lifetime of desire, he had the chance to take his vengeance for the wrongdoing.

A gusting wind brought raindrops as large and hard as peas to drum against his face, and Hacon swept a hand across before flicking the water away; turning his back to the downpour he gazed down the slope to the bedraggled army lined up at its foot. Duke William was in plain sight, cajoling his closest companions into attacking again, and Hacon marked their armour so that he would easily recognise each man should they venture within the swing of his axe: Odo, bishop of Bayeux; William FitzOsbern; Turstin son of Rollo beneath the papal banner; Walter Giffard....

Spooning another mouthful, he reflected on the hectic month he had just lived through as the Normans reformed their battles and prepared to attack again. Four weeks previously it had seemed as though the great invasion scare of 1066 had been just that, a scare. After a summer spent scanning the horizon from the clifftops of the southern coastline, the king had released the levy men of the fyrd as harvest time arrived with no sign of the promised holt of masts. Leaving only a token force on watch, the king had released his southern thegns and returned to London with his housecarls. Only a madman would cross the channel so late in the year, and Hacon had advised his uncle the king that duke William was anything but.

But the Lord was not yet finished with the English that year and in mid September Harald Sigurdsson, king of Norway, had appeared in the North with yet another of his uncles, the king's brother Tostig. Moving on York they had swept the army of the northern earls aside. Message bearers had arrived in London around the same time that the armies had clashed outside the city, and the king had hurried to reinforce his loyal countrymen. Men had flocked to his banner as the army sped north, gathering strength as men grasped the chance to repay the Vikings for centuries of wrongs. Arriving like a thunderbolt from the summer sky they had fallen upon the Norwegians and all but annihilated them, but as the army had retired to York to celebrate the victory and honour the dead, a messenger had hurried in from the South. The wind had finally turned and William had seized his chance. King Harold had gathered the cream of his army, the mounted housecarls and thegns, and set off back along the Great North Road.

But the same westerlies which had carried the invasion fleet to the coast of Sussex had also brought the first heavy rains of autumn in their wake. Penned in against the marshes and lagoons by the dense woodland of Andredes Weald the Norman army had begun to flounder almost immediately. Utilising their local knowledge to the full the southern thegns had shadowed the force, and soon they were witnessing the first Normans succumb to the bloody flux. Illness and fever had risen wraith like from the marshlands, and within days the invaders had begun to cut the seat of their breeches away in a desperate attempt to ease their discomfort. Fearful of moving away from the sea and his only source of reinforcement, the duke had hesitated to venture inland. King Harold had gathered his force in London and bided his time as the enemy grew weaker with each passing day, and finally God had rewarded his patience. Desperate to escape the fetid marshlands and safeguard his coastal supply line, the duke had withdrawn his army to Hastings. Word had quickly reached the king in London and he had seized the opportunity. Moving south the English army had thrown itself across the Hastings road, the only route out of the peninsula, as the fyrdmen of the southern shires had flocked to reinforce them. The fighting that day had been hard as the Normans fought to escape the trap. But the shield wall had held, and each attack had been turned back with increasing ease as the invaders tired and fresh men arrived to bolster the English line.

The rain redoubled, and Hacon drew in his head in a vain attempt at keeping the icy fingers from penetrating his neckband. The deluge had persisted for most of the day and he was soaked through; now the wind gusted to add to their discomfort, howling through the grove of trees which anchored the battle line at each end of the ridge as if God and his angels were mourning the day that Christian men hewed each other to bloodied corpses.

The strident call of battle horns chased away his daydreams, and Hacon glanced down at the enemy. The Duke was hauling himself into the saddle, and Sweyn's son watched as the gaily coloured war flags and *gonfanon* he knew so well curled and snapped in the freshening wind. As the Norman foot soldiers shuffled back into line, Hacon glanced back to the west and saw that the wan light which marked the position of the sun was now barely above the woodland backing Telham Hill. The shadows were lengthening quickly in the valley below and every man — Norman, Dane, French and English — knew that this must be the final desperate charge of the day.

Hacon hefted his Dane axe, rolling his shoulders as the distant figure raised its sword and urged the ragged army forward. Fourteen years he had spent as an unwilling guest of the duke, years in which he had grown from childhood to manhood, and he hawked and spat his disdain for the shining figure in the valley as he took his place in the battle line.

WILLIAM CRANED forward over the neck of the war horse, hunkering into his shield as he spurred the beast up the rise. Ahead of him he could see his adversary beneath the twin banners which had tormented him throughout that long day, safely ensconced within a protective fort of housecarls and thegns. The usurper's personal banner, the golden warrior called the Fighting Man he had recognised from Harold's time in his duchy, but the Wessex Dragon was new to him, and he had resolved earlier that this would be the last time that it would fly over an English army, ancient symbol or not.

The Duke risked a glance to his left at the bulk of his army, cursing as he saw that they had barely begun to climb the escarpment. The valley side had cut up badly during the course of the fighting, as the repeated attacks of the foot soldiers and mounted knights churned up the grassy banks. The slope was fully in shade now as daylight fled the land, and William knew that he must kill Harold this time or lose everything.

Horses edged to his side, and he saw that Hugh of Ponthieu and Walter Giffard had taken up position on his flanks in support. Sure now of the Norman tactics, the English would wait until they turned off the roadway to run side-on to their shield wall before they moved forward to hack at the flanks with their murderous axes. But the Normans too had learnt that day, and this attack would be different. No horse could be made to run directly into a solid wall of snarling men any more than it would a tree, but they were herd animals and they would blindly follow the leading stallion if denied the chance to make a decision for themselves. A well trained *destrier* could be trained to shoulder his way into a battle line and William's mount was one such horse, the finest on the field.

Curbing the reins, William began to check the headlong rush of the animal as the English shields came up, and raising his long spear he took up the overarm stance which he knew the enemy would now expect him to take. It was the sign that he was about to work his way along the front ranks as he stabbed down above the shields and attempted to break their formation, before wheeling away to circle back and try again. As the enemy brought their shields up to cover their heads William struck, gripping his reins tightly as he urged the horse on into the dense hedge of shields, spear points and axes. The ruse worked beyond his wildest hopes, and taken by surprise the defenders were bowled aside as the horse shouldered its way deep into the English ranks. William snatched a look ahead. His mad dash had brought him almost within reach of the man who wore the crown which was rightfully his, and the duke felt a kick of excitement as he skewered a housecarl, leaving the spear imbedded in the Englishman to draw his sword as he cleared the densely packed front ranks and guided the horse towards the Fighting Man.

The raindrops stung his face as he broke free from the cover of the hill and came into the full force of the gale, and he desperately blinked away the water as it threatened to blind him. Walter Giffard was still at his side, and although Hugh of Ponthieu was suddenly unhorsed and disappeared from view, the mount kept pace with their own and continued to shield William's charge. Behind him he knew that the Norman wedge would be pushing forward through the crush as others poured into the breach, widening it with every passing moment, and with victory finally within his grasp he looked on, elated, as Harold drew his sword and prepared to defend himself.

No man could have hoped to survive as long as he had as duke of the Normans without developing an awareness of imminent danger, and William flicked a look across to his left as he sensed it now. Among the men who were fighting desperately to remake the battle line following his irresistible charge, William blinked in surprise as he recognised an axeman shouldering his way through the crowd. The Sweynson brat was a few yards away, moving forward with purpose, and the duke raised his shield to deflect the blow as Hacon cried the name of his cousin and swung.

THE NORMAN CHARGE was almost upon them, and Hacon shifted his grip on the haft of the axe as men to either side raised shields and hurled their insults. The duke himself was leading this attack, flanked by Walter Giffard and yet another French bastard, Hugh of Ponthieu, and he took a last look to the south as he sought to reassure himself that all was well there. As he had expected the Norman foot soldiers were barely half way up the hill, slipping and sliding as their bodies, already weakened by weeks of illness and fever struggled to make headway on the slick ground underfoot. The valley side had become a quagmire over the course of the day as attack followed attack, and the Norman horse had been pushed further and further to the North where the English straddled the only road out of the peninsula. By mid afternoon it was clear that the clinging mud on the valley slope was becoming almost impassable to the enemy, and king Harold had shifted his own position across to bolster the left wing as the Normans began to concentrate the attacks there.

Despite the difficulties, every Norman assault that day had been a carefully orchestrated affair, each element working in mutual support, and Hacon suddenly realised that this was different. By beginning his attack at the same time as the foot soldiers and leading his knights up the Hastings road, they would reach the English position long before the supporting spearmen could arrive. Either the Norman duke had lost control of his army or the plan had changed. He of course knew not only duke William, but the majority of the Norman leaders: they were calculating men, men not given to hasty action or desperate gambles. As his comrades locked shields and prepared to receive the attack, Hacon hung back and watched.

Still waiting for the Normans to struggle up the slope, the English warriors were clashing their weapons against the boards of their shields and hurling abuse. The age-old rhythmic chant of the English army rolled out through the dusk at their approach, *Ut!-Ut!-Ut! — Get out of my land!* and the young Sweynson, convinced now that the Normans had changed their tactics began to drift instinctively towards his king. Hacon fixed his eyes upon the duke as he walked, the lion flag of Normandy which marked his coming bone-fire red in the dusk, but although the enemy leader raised his spear high to stab into English faces in the same old way there was something in his movements which gave them the lie. A moment later his fears were confirmed as the duke tugged at the reins, angling the horse to meet the defenders head on. Hugh of Ponthieu and Walter Giffard were at the duke's shoulders, and as the trio spurred their mounts deeper into the English defence Hacon watched in horror as the shield wall, impregnable throughout that dank autumn day, finally lost its cohesion. A flash of steel away to the left showed where the king's housecarls had recognised the threat, raising their axe blades as one, and as king Harold drew his sword and began to move against the foe, Hacon locked his gaze on the duke and shouldered his way through the crush.

A spearman darted in, skewering Hugh of Ponthieu and sending the knight flying from the saddle as if snatched away by the hand of a giant. Run through by several spearmen as he fell count Guy's brother was swallowed by the crowd, but his horse, unable to turn away from the mass of men amid the sky ripping clamour of battle came on regardless.

Hacon was almost up with the attackers now, and he shoved men aside as his eyes remained locked upon the duke. The riderless horse slowed and veered away as a gap in the mad scrum opened up before it, and Hacon gripped the haft of his war axe and wound his body as a clear path to the duke presented itself. Something, a sense of unseen danger, caused duke William to shoot a look in his direction; Hacon ensured he would be recognised as he roared his cousin's name and the Dane axe swept down:

'Wulfnoth!'

William's eyes reflected the fury of battle as he angled his shield to parry the strike, but Hacon felt a stab of triumph as he saw that his old gaoler had misjudged where the blow would fall. As William's shield came up the Englishman's axe blade sang its death song as it cut the air, and the moment duke William was unsighted Hacon dipped a shoulder to alter its trajectory. Honed to a perfect cutting edge the blade slowed for a heartbeat as it connected with the horse's nape and then it was through, slicing down through spine, muscle and tendon to emerge in a wellspring of blood. Hacon sprang back as the mortally wounded horse thundered past, narrowly dodging the duke's retaliatory sword swing, and he watched transfixed as the war horse slowed and its forelegs folded. As the horse crashed to the turf the duke was thrown from the saddle, and before he could recover he was pinned to the ground by a knot of baying spearmen.

Satisfied that the enemy leader was taken Hacon turned away. The defenders were fighting hard to close the breach, spear points and sword blades glinting in the dying light; Walter Giffard was attempting to ride to his lord's rescue, but the press of Englishmen was forcing his mount to a standstill and within moments an axe blade hooked his shoulder and the Norman began to fall. Giffard was an old enemy from their youth together in Normandy, and the chance to settle old scores had Hacon running across to be in at the kill. A glance towards the battle line showed that the Norman knights were being slaughtered as word of their leader's fall spread, each man looking to extricate himself from the melee as panic gripped them.

Walter Giffard finally slid from view, the knight's expression a mask of horror and disbelief as an English spear pricked his guts, and Hacon thrilled at the sight of so many of the men who had thought themselves his betters finding their death on a rain lashed English hillside. As he drew nearer it became clear to Hacon that the short time it had taken to cross to the place where the knight had fallen had cost him his chance. The men there were already straightening their backs as they prepared to return to the fight, and Hacon marked the death wounds with relish as he recalled the man's taunts and loftiness of old. A red gash marked where a sword had cut through the mail shirt to open his enemy's chest; beneath this another had opened his belly, the ropes of blue-grey guts spilling out to steam in the cool air. Beheaded and eviscerated as he was Walter Giffard now resembled a slaughtered hog, and in a final indignity Hacon looked on as a spearman drew a knife to emasculate the corpse before turning to throw the handful of gore over the heads of the shield wall to land among the last of the Norman horsemen. It was the final act of the day as they took the unmistakable parts to have belonged to the duke, and within moments they had hauled at their reins and spurred back down the slope.

As the knights retreated and the English ranks came back together a great rolling roar shattered the gathering dusk, and Hacon shared looks of joy with those nearby as it became clear that word of the duke's fall was moving like a brush fire along the length of the ridge top host. Hacon had little doubt that the whole of duke William's army was now streaming back down the slope, desperately attempting to regain the coast before news of the disaster reached the ship masters and they cut their cables and ran. A familiar voice sounded at his shoulder then, and he turned to smile at the king.

'Hacon Sweynson,' Harold said. 'You have fulfilled your oath, and the duke is our captive — the day is ours.'

Ansgar the Staller was alongside the king, the Fighting Man war banner a swatch of gold and blue in a darkening sky. Beyond them the dragons of Wessex dominated the skyline as they had throughout that tempestuous day.

The king spoke again. 'I will be needing a trusted man to keep an eye on our honoured guest,' he said with a backwards glance. 'While I negotiate a suitable ransom and arrange the return of our kinsman Wulfnoth.'

King Harold smiled again. 'I rather thought that you might like to be that man?'

AFTERWORD

In addition to the widely reported role which the prevailing winds played that summer by bottling up the Norman fleet, remarkably we have a first hand account of the actual weather conditions in the channel during the late summer and autumn of 1066. Although the *Carmen de Hastingae Proelio*, the *Song of the Battle of Hastings*, was a late discovery (it was found in the Royal Library in Brussels in 1826) it is almost certainly the work of Guy, bishop of Amiens. The later historian Orderic Vitalis tells us that the poem was written in the spring of 1068, not much more than a year and a half after the battle itself, for the entertainment of the now King William of England. In it we have the description of the weather in the early weeks of September: 'It was cold and wet,' Guy writes, 'and the sky was hidden by clouds and rain.' Even today those months can be among the most changeable in England and Atlantic storms can, and do, batter the country at any time of the year with the autumn months being especially prone.

Having visited the battlefield myself, it is easy to see the effect that hundreds of horses and thousands of heavily armed men would have on the area following even a few days of heavy rain. Several of the present day re-enactments which are held at the abbey close to the anniversary of the battle itself have been cancelled as rain turned the valley into a mud bath.

In reality, William had three horses killed from under him during the battle and the Norman army and their allies very nearly broke and ran. The Bayeux tapestry depicts the moment when William was forced to lift his helm and ride around the field of battle to counter rumours that he had died. William gambled and won — it could so easily have been very different.

The Hacon Sweynson of our tale was the only known child of the eldest of earl Godwin's sons. Sweyn Godwinson was a bit of a rogue who managed to get himself exiled from England three times, and Denmark once, within the space of five years. During this time he also murdered his cousin Beorn who was attempting to help him gain a pardon from king Edward, and abducted the abbess of Leominster, a lady called Eadgifu, who he seems to have intended to marry to gain control of the abbey's lands. He in turn was murdered returning from pilgrimage to Jerusalem in 1052, and I have taken Eadgifu to be the mother of young Hacon which would make him nineteen or twenty years old in 1066. The events which led to the banishment of the Godwin clan in 1051 and their return to England the following year are outlined in *Peace Weaver* so I shan't go into detail here, but young Hacon along with his cousin Wulfnoth were initially handed over as hostages and then spirited away to Normandy — probably by Robert of Jumièges, the fleeing archbishop of Canterbury. Harold retrieved Hacon from captivity in 1064, but was unable to rescue his young brother Wulfnoth who was destined to remain a prisoner until his death at

Winchester in 1094. Having grown up together in a foreign land, it seems highly likely that Hacon would want to fight both against his long-term captors and to win the freedom of his kinsman and fellow detainee, and so I made him the hero of our story.

Several Norman sources describe the death of King Harold and the knights responsible and I have used them here. The king's reported death wounds I have transferred to Walter Giffard.

Only a handful of names other than Harold and his brothers have come down to us from the thousands of Englishmen who fought and died on that fateful day. Were it not for chance mentions in legal documents, the Anglo-Saxon Chronicle or Domesday Book we should barely know a single one. To honour them and the men who fell at their side, I will list those which I came across during my research for this book:

Harold Godwinson - King of England

Gyrth Godwinson - Earl of East Anglia

Leofwine Godwinson - Earl of Middlesex

Thurkill of Kingston, Berkshire

Esegar, shire reeve of Middlesex

Ælfwig, Abbot of Winchester - An uncle of the king, the Warenne Chronicle *tells us he fought alongside twelve of his monks, all clad in mail*

Shire reeve Godric, Lord of Fifhide, Berkshire

Ansgar the Staller, port reeve of London and shire reeve of Middlesex. Mortally wounded at Hastings, Ansgar may have been King Harold's standard bearer at the battle

Eadric the deacon, a landowner at Cavendish, Suffolk

Ælfwold, abbot

Ælfric, thegn of Huntingdonshire

Skalpi - A housecarl owning lands held directly from Harold straddling the Suffolk/Essex border

Alwi of Thetford, Norfolk

Ringolf of Oby

Breme of Suffolk

An unnamed Freeman of Harold's from Cavendish in Suffolk

An Englishman known only as a "son of Helloc"

A nameless tenant who is recorded in Domesday Book holding 12 acres worth 16 pennies at Bury St Edmunds, Suffolk

Again from Domesday Book - two unnamed men (brothers? friends?) who held land in Tytherley, Hampshire

4

EARL HAROLD'S WAR

The old man teased the strands of his beard, settling back with a weary sigh as he turned his gaze to the nearby window. The trees outside were dark hands against a hard magenta sky as the harsh winter of 1094 gripped the land.

The journey up from London had been a hard day's ride, and guilt had chivvied his conscience at the sight of his sons and grandsons spurring the horses through banks of drifting snow. But they were here now, the fires were roaring, the drink flowing, and the sounds of laughter and merriment drifting in from the hall beyond reminded him of his own youth. He leaned forward once again, squinting as he ran a bony finger down the page of the chronicle. 'Now, where was I?'

Harold chuckled as he remembered where he had left off, and he slid the tip of a forefinger across the words as he recalled the events of that tumultuous year. 'Ah yes, of course, you silly old fool — 1066, how could you forget?'

The metallic clack of a latch interrupted the earl before he could begin, and he glanced across as one of the brothers entered with a respectful bob of the head. 'Excuse me, lord,' he said with a smile. 'I have come to light the candles and tend to the hearth.'

Harold returned the smile, nodding his assent as the old cleric shuffled in. The brothers at Waltham always doted on their most distinguished visitor and he snorted at it. *And so they should. Not only have I paid practically all of their costs for the past forty years, I have endowed the abbey with more holy relics than West Minster!*

As the churchman fussed around him and the evening shadows retreated to the furthest corners of the room, the old earl propped the ancient book, leaned in and began to read:

1066

As related, King Edward came to Westminster at Christmas, and there let the minster be hallowed that he himself built, to the glory of God and all God's saints.

He remained there into this year and passed away on twelfth night, being interred on twelfth day in the same minster. Edward, king, lord of the English, sent his soul, strong in truth, to Christ. In God's safekeeping, his holy spirit. The wise one committed the kingdom to one in high rank,

Harold, noble earl, who at all times faithfully obeyed his lord in words and deeds, holding back nothing at the need of the king and people.

Harold smiled his thanks as the clergyman recharged his cup and left the room. Taking up the drink, the old earl chuckled again as he recalled the faces of the *witan,* the wise men, when he had refused to accept the kingly gift. True, he was the only Englishman who could possibly defend the country from the rival claimants to the throne. Although descended from the old West Saxon line of kings, Edgar ætheling was a stripling and thought not yet ready for the rigours of kingship.

Harold sipped his ale, congratulating himself as he came to the same conclusion which he had reached almost thirty years previously.

King Edward was growing old in years, and the succession had been uppermost on his mind. He had prayed for guidance at the chapel in Bosham, before setting out on a simple fishing trip along the coast. The Lord had sent a squall which blew them across the channel and he had come into the power of the duke. He had been treated with honour and they had quickly become friends. After witnessing the might of the Norman army and the qualities of their ruler in a campaign against the Bretons, he had recognised that this had been no chance meeting but God's will and willingly promised to support William's claim to his cousin, King Edward's, throne. Despite the secrecy of their pact, William had promised before witnesses on holy relics that no English lord or churchman would be forcibly replaced on his accession, and that English laws and customs would be safeguarded. Harold had been confirmed in his earldom of Wessex and the ætheling, Edgar, was to be declared William's chosen heir in England. It had been the greatest service he had ever given his countrymen.

His finger ran on down the yellowing vellum, the earl muttering as it did so: 'long-haired star...crowned King William at West Minster...earl Tostig came into the Humber with sixty ships...ah, here it is — Earl Harold's War.'

King Harald Sigurdsson of Norway came to this land with a force of three hundred ships.

Earl Tostig submitted to Harald and became his man,

and together they went up into the Humber until they came to York, and fought with them there, earl Edwin and earl Morcar his brother; and the Norwegians had the victory.

Earl Harold, who the Normans called sub-regulus but his own people the shepherd of the English, was informed that this had befallen; king William having returned then to Normandy.

Earl Harold gathered together a great host of English folk and those men of Normandy who were on this side of the sea and came against the Norwegians at the River Trent.

There was that day fought a very great battle. King Harald, whom the Norwegians named Hardrada for his ruthlessness, fell there with a very great number of his host and the earl Tostig taken. The Norwegians who remained were put to flight and the Norman knights pursued them from the field, hewing at them from behind so that few reached the safety of their ships, and the army of earl Harold held the field of slaughter.

Then the earl went up to the Humber and offered terms to the son of the king of Norway. Olaf swore oaths that he would forever hold peace and friendship with this land and the earl let him sail home with twenty ships.

Harold, earl of Wessex, sent word to the king in Normandy of his overwhelming victory and King William held the earl to be the greatest of his subjects.

Harold's features mirrored the peculiar feelings of pride and horror which swept through him each time that he read the passage. The brothers at the abbey, rightly, were proud of their benefactor and his achievement. It had been his greatest day, and the monks had listened to his recollections and faithfully captured the essence of the triumph in the chronicle.

The earl sighed and looked out once again across the

abbey grounds to the dark outline of the woodland beyond. A murder of crows was circling above an ancient oak, the harshness of their cawing adding a sense of eeriness as the screams and cries of the battlefield returned to haunt Harold's mind. No words, however cunningly crafted, could convey the sheer horror of that day. The deafening crash as thousands of shields came together, spear points glinting in the summer sun, the rise and fall of silvered blades as they chopped at steel and flesh. The sky had darkened as Mercian, Welsh and Norman arrows had whispered overhead to take the rear ranks of the Vikings. And then without warning the Norsemen had broken, streaming away to leave the line of their dead and the smell of blood, gore and loosened bowels to mark the high tide of their advance.

The old man closed his eyes as he attempted to block out the shrieks and yells, but all he heard was the thunderous pounding of hooves. His friend, William Mallet, had led the knights of Normandy around the flanks of the allied shield wall and chased the Norwegians from the field. Trapped with their backs to the River Trent, they had thrown themselves into the flood in their terror. Harold had walked down to the place later that day and watched scores of English and Normans laughing together as they crossed and recrossed the river on a bridge of bodies.

The memories had drawn the enjoyment from the moment and the earl quickly ran his finger down the page. He recovered his humour as he did so, smiling here and there as the tale of his life unfolded in the lines before him until only blank parchment remained. Closing the ancient tome with a soft thud, he rose and carried it across to the scribe sat patiently waiting at the desk the brothers now called an *escritoire* after the fashion of their Norman brethren. Harold felt the merest pang of regret at the intrusion; he was too old now to change his ways, he still preferred the old English word *tabule.*

Brother Wigstan smiled self-consciously and handed across a loose leaf. Holed and grimy the edges were roughly fashioned, and Harold could see that the words written there were obviously a working draft.

Wigstan blinked nervously at the grizzled old warrior. 'Would you care to approve my work before I begin to transcribe the words into the chronicle, lord?'

Harold nodded that he would, moved closer to the candle and began to read.

This year William, king, lord of the English and Normans, sent his soul to Christ, in God's safekeeping, his holy spirit.

He in this world dwelt for a time in kingly power and wise council, a just man but fierce; no man dared against his will.

He had castles built to thwart the Dane and any foreign prince who coveted this land,

Wales was in his power; he built castles therein, and ruled all the people there.

So also Scotland he subjected by his great strength.

Normandy was his natural land, and over the earldom called Maine he reigned.

Among other things it is not to be forgotten, that good peace he made in this land, so that a man of any account might fare over the kingdom with a bosom full of gold unmolested; and no man dared kill another man, even if he had done much evil to him; and if any man lay with a woman against her will, he soon lost those limbs he played with.

William, who the English called the good, defended his

home, land and people, until suddenly came death; the angels accompanied him, into the sky's light.

And so all folk received Edgar as king, as was his natural right.

He was hallowed at West Minster with much celebration, and Archbishop Eadmer instructed him well before all the folk, and reminded him of his duties towards the welfare of all the people.

Harold raised his eyes, smiling at the almost childlike anticipation painted on the face of the scribe as he waited for the venerable earl's verdict on his handiwork. The words would be read by the great, great grandchildren of men not yet born, and the weight of responsibility was obviously weighing heavily on the younger man.

'Yes, I like it,' Harold said after a pause to reflect on the greatness of his friend the king. 'I like it a lot.'

AFTERWORD

Harold Godwinson was the wealthiest and most powerful man in the kingdom at the time of the death of Edward the Confessor on 5 January 1066, but does that necessarily mean that he coveted the throne itself?

All contemporary chroniclers praise Harold for his loyalty towards King Edward. There is evidence that Harold was heavily involved in bringing back Edward the Exile from Hungary (see *The Exile*), and even references to Harold in Norman sources grudgingly admit his qualities. Harold and William knew each other well. There was an unexplained voyage in 1064 which resulted in Harold campaigning alongside the Norman army against the Bretons. Harold impressed the Normans, and an incident of personal bravery is commemorated on the Bayeux tapestry itself.

That Harold and William held one another in mutual respect I think is reflected in the number of times that William sent messengers to Harold asking him to relinquish the throne in 1066. Even after the duke had landed in England he let it be known that the way was still open to a negotiated settlement, and a Norman knight who desecrated Harold's body on the battlefield was sent away in disgrace. William saw himself as the rightful king, and had intended to rule as king of the English as traditionally as he was able. Even after Hastings he confirmed the majority of those who had not actively fought against him in their titles and offices, and it was only after the ongoing rebellions of the following years culminating in the rising in the North which hardened his attitude. That he refrained from killing Edgar ætheling despite his repeated betrayals (a man who after all had a better claim to the kingship) when it was in his power to do so supports this.

Did Harold swear in Normandy on holy relics to support William's claim to the throne? Yes, I believe there is little doubt that he did, but I also think that William recognised that Harold had been placed in a difficult position at the time of king Edward's death. Despite Edward's likely bequeathal of the kingship in 1051, William was a realist who knew that there was no pro-Norman faction in England. Even after the defeat of Harold's army at Hastings, the duke waited in vain for a delegation to arrive from London to offer him the crown.

Maybe Harold *was* content to leave ultimate rule to others if they were prepared in turn to guarantee his own earldom and those of his brothers, but was pressed by the Witan to take the crown as the only suitable English candidate in a time of crisis. Harold may well have worked loyally in support of King William, as his own father Godwin had done for several kings; it had been after all, the means by which the family had risen from obscurity to unimaginable wealth and power in little more than half a century.

5

ASSASSINS

THE KEEP OF LE VAUDREUIL CASTLE
WINTER 1040

The log settled with a crack, sending a plume of sparks billowing. Osbern was awake in an instant, and he tensed in the dark as his ears strained to pick up the slightest sound. A faint light showed beneath the heavy oak door, and the comforting shadow cast by the guard who patrolled the passageway outside slid across it as the man continued his nocturnal watch.

The seneschal slowly uncurled his fingers from the sword grip and lay back with a sigh. Five years had passed since the old duke had died on his return trip from Jerusalem, and the duchy was still in chaos. It sometimes appeared as if every baron and knight, within the borders of Normandy and without, were either in active revolt or scheming among themselves for the ultimate prize of winning the title Duke of the Normans for himself.

The wind outside the keep whistled and howled around its sturdy battlements, and Osbern reached across to run a hand lightly across the dips and mounds of the woman at his side. She purred in her sleep, prompting a predatory smile: could he wait until morning? Reassured now that all was well his mind drifted back to the first time he had laid eyes upon her as he drew back the cover to drink in her beauty. Crossing the little River Charentonne in company with his closest men he had stumbled upon the woman bathing in the clear waters, and he recalled her efforts to cover the fullness of her breasts with handfuls of pondweed with a chuckle of delight. Luck had deserted her that day. Very few people knew that the local lord used the shallows there as a shortcut home, but learning that she had been newly widowed the seneschal had offered her a place in his household. It was one of the best decisions he had made he snorted, as he watched the down on the small of her back stiffen in the cool night air. She had certainly shed any feelings of bashfulness once he had taken her to his bed. Osbern's hand moved to gently cup the smoothness of a buttock as her scent excited his senses, but an instant later his desire fled as a sound from the passageway caused him to freeze. There were two types of nobles in Normandy — those who could sniff out danger in their sleep or even in the throes of passion and the dead, and he listened hard as the girl shifted beside him. There it was again: a slight murmur. He recognised the sound for what it was, and slipping from the bed crept across to the archway which led to the small room adjoining his own. A quick glance back at the door confirmed his fears as he saw the unmistakable flurry of shadows which marked the death of his guard. Turning quickly, he called into the small bed chamber. 'Duke William, arm yourself, we are under attack!'

Despite his years, the duke was awake in an instant. Springing from his bed he took up his sword and fixed his guardian with a penetrating stare.

'Numbers?'

The seneschal shook his head and tried to encourage the boy with a grim smile. 'Your loyal men will arrive before they can break in, but if they do we shall strike them down and make a heap of their bodies together. Remember our plan, lord. I shall defend this portal, and you fight like a Duke of Normandy should I fall.'

William nodded, his eyes bright with excitement. Now a man of ten full years, he relished the opportunity to kill those who wished him harm.

Osbern reached out to the bell which he kept beside the settle for just such emergencies, but to his surprise he found that he was clutching at air. Irritated by his clumsiness, he cast a look back at the main door as he heard the handle turn. It would do them little good. The door was as thick as his arm and made of good seasoned oak, while the hinges on which such a stout door was hung could suspend a horse. The locking bar would hold them, and soon the tolling of the bell would alert his men who would race to snuff out the danger.

Osbern gasped in horror at the scene which greeted him: *'No!'*

The beam had already been removed and stood propped against the wall of the chamber, the bell resting mutely at its side. The woman was already reaching out to turn the key in the lock as the shadows gathered on the far side.

As the seneschal braced himself to receive the attack he knew in his heart that he had failed his lord, that the young duke would fall. It was the futile last action of a dead man.

THE MIDNIGHT RIDE

The guard paused as if hoping the man at his shoulder would disappear, before making a fist to tap on the boards of the door. He threw the slight figure a sidelong look, all of his fears revealed in the glance as the sound reverberated along the passageway. 'This information had better be reliable,' he growled. 'Waking the duke after a long day in the saddle, and on the say-so of a jongleur!' Walter shook his head as his knuckles came up to rap the boards a little louder. 'If this is some kind of joke, you will need more than fine words and merry tunes to recover your bladder-on-a-stick from where I will be shoving it.'

The guard paused, cocking an ear as close to the duke's door as he dare. It was bad enough that he had drawn the first watch after a day hunt, the thought of his lord throwing the door open with his ear pressed against it would just about make the night complete. Walter glared at the harlequin as the time to make a decision arrived, before sliding his eyes across to look at the spearmen flanking the doorway. 'Remain here with these boys,' he said, 'unless either myself or Duke William calls you into the chamber.' Without waiting for a reply, the big Norman turned the handle and slipped into the room. A shadow detached itself from a corner, the accompanying growl rooting him to the spot as the wolfhound lowered his head and slunk across. Walter clicked his tongue, opening a hand to allow the dog to catch his scent as his eyes slowly adjusted to the gloom. The fire against the sidewall cast a crimson glow across the chamber, the guttering flames breathing life into the men and beasts adorning the wall hangings.

The wolfhound reached him, and Walter purred the dog's name as the damp nose came up to sniff. The noise at last woke the sole occupant from his slumber, and man and dog instinctively drew themselves upright as the duke's legs swung clear of the bed and his hand closed about the handle of his sword. 'Who is it?'

The guard cleared his throat. 'It is Walter de Lacey, lord. There is a man here who says he has uncovered a plot against your life.'

Despite the intrusion, William snorted as he knuckled the sleep from his eyes. 'That is hardly news Walter, could it not wait until morning?'

'He says not, lord. He assures me that you are in great danger.'

William nodded, tossing his sword on the bed as he reached for a gown. 'Is this fellow known to us?'

Walter's heart sank, but he had come this far and there was no going back. 'It's the jongleur the men call Ivo, lord.'

The Duke thought for a moment as he sought to place the name. Then he had it. 'Taillefer you mean? The gleeman whose favourite recital is the Song of Roland?'

Walter nodded. 'That's him, the one with the funny stick.' He pulled a face. 'He was very insistent, lord.'

William nodded. 'I will see him.'

The duke turned aside, moving across to fill a cup from the side board as his bodyguard drew the door inward and motioned with his head. William savoured the feeling of the mead as it went down; the hunt had been a success: deer; fowl; even a boar had fallen to their lances and arrows. The night had been long and raucous despite their tiredness, as the men had feasted on the flesh of their quarry and drunk deep into the night.

Taillifer hurried in, a little too fast for the dog whose raised hackles and low growl were enough to check his stride, but a moment later the man was on one knee as he bent his head in supplication and the dog bared its fangs and circled. William ran his eyes over the figure before him as he drained the cup. Still in his performing clothes he looked travel-worn and dishevelled, and the distinctive smell of a horse run hard came from him. If it was a trick it was a well thought through one, and the duke felt the first feelings of alarm as he indicated that the man rise and speak.

'My duke, my beloved lord,' the man blurted. 'Men are on their way to kill you. They are not far behind me, you must look to your defence.'

Duke William sensed Walter begin to move, but he held up a hand to stay him. Nobody gave the duke of Normandy orders, save perhaps King Henry, his liege lord in far-off Paris, but this duke had not survived nigh on twenty years and several assassination attempts without developing a sense of impending danger. He was deep within the Cotentin, an area his spies had already warned him was becoming a hotbed of resistance to his rule under the prodding of Guy, the count of Burgundy. Maybe he had underestimated just how advanced their plans had become? William forced his voice to remain calm as his mind began to reckon the number of soldiers available to him, cursing the decision which had let his supporters and their valuable soldiery return to their castles following the feasting. 'From whence have you come, Taillefer?' he said. 'Tell me all you know.'

The minstrel was clearly distressed and he began to repeat his earlier plea, but his sense of duty reasserted itself before William could intervene, and the duke listened with growing alarm as the man recounted his tale. 'I was the entertainer at Le Homme castle, my lord. A minstrel hears many things when wine loosens tongues, and I listened in as the following men pledged their forces and toasted your downfall.' William shared a look of concern with Walter as Taillefer reeled off a list of the most important men in the area. 'They are led by Count Guy of Brionne who aims to take the duchy for himself. The other conspirators present were: Nigel, count of Cotentin; Rannulf, count of Bessin; Haimo Dentatus and

Grimoult du Plessis. I thought to rise early and warn you on the morrow, but all of a sudden du Plessis jumps up and declares that he will do the deed tonight. The hall was in uproar my duke as he and his men made ready to leave, so it was easy for a humble entertainer to slip away in the din.' Taillifer fixed the duke with a look, and the fear reflected in his gaze convinced William that the man told the truth. 'I urge you to wake the garrison lord, the horses were being saddled as I left, they cannot be far behind me.'

William shot a look at Walter. 'How many men do we have here?'

'No more than a score, lord,' he answered sadly. 'The castle was too small to house more with the numbers of guests we were to entertain following the hunt.'

William nodded as he slipped into his leggings. 'That is too few to withstand a siege, we shall ride for home. Bring my boots and gather the men.' His decision made, the duke moved with speed. Taking the stone steps two at a time, he was crossing the bailey to the stable block when he was approached by one of his guards. 'The man on the walkway reports horsemen on the northern road, lord,' the sentinel reported, 'maybe a mile off and heading this way. Judging by the moonlight reflecting from mail and helm he puts their number at three score or more.'

The duke stole a glance at the night sky. A gibbous moon shone brightly in a firmament awash with stars, and he sent a prayer of thanks to the Lord in Heaven that he had seen fit to aid him in his struggle.

The guard was speaking again. 'I have taken the liberty of ordering the horses saddled, lord. We await your orders.' The heavy stomp of booted feet caused the duke to turn back. His soldiery were emerging from the doorway in various stages of undress as the sleep befuddled men pulled on mail and buckled sword belts. Walter was at their head, his lord's riding boots in his hand, but the chill of cold stone on the soles of his feet was forgotten as the man stopped and cocked an ear. The courtyard grew still as men paused to listen, and expressions of alarm replaced heavy-eyed looks as the thud of hoofbeats carried to them on the still air. Walter's eyes widened in dread. 'Ride, lord!' he exclaimed. 'We will hold them off for as long as we can, and make our own way back.'

It took only a moment of hesitation before the duke saw the wisdom in his friend's words, and he nodded gravely as the mount was led across and he hauled himself into the saddle. 'Disrupt their charge and make your escape,' he called as he dragged the head of his horse towards the castle gate. He swept the compound with a final look as his heels went back to urge his mount on. 'They will not be expecting to face opposition on the road and will quickly lose heart; strike like a thunderbolt and make for Falaise.' He reiterated his order as the horse passed into the shadow cast by the barbican. They were among the best of his men and he would need them for the coming war. 'Remember, no unnecessary heroics. Go in hard, scatter them and make your way south.'

Walter's voice was the last thing he heard as the horse passed through the archway, the familiar gruffness comforting to the young duke as the woodland which gird the fortress came into view. William pulled at the reins, pausing the horse as it came onto the moon washed castle approach. Like many such strong points Castle Valognes had been constructed at a strategic crossing point, the place where the main routes led away to east and west, north and south. The clatter of hoofbeats came clearly now from the North: safety lay to the South, but if that was obvious to him he had to assume that it would be just as plain to his enemies. He recalled a smaller pathway leading southwestwards, the meandering route little more than a country track a little way along the main route south, and he clicked his horse on as he realised that he had little option; he would have to take the chance that no riders had been sent on ahead to block any retreat.

The first of his men were exiting the barbican, Walter de Lacey's armour sword blade bright in the moonlight as he took the northern road, but William was already back in the shadows and increasing the pace. The duke urged the horse into a steady canter, mindful that he would need to set a steady gait if they were to ride through the night and reach the safety of Falaise. The roadway stretched away, iron grey in the gloom, and within half a mile William saw the gnarled oak, bent backed and twisted like an aged crone, which marked the entrance to the woodland path. Moments later he was within its welcome embrace, and although the darkness forced him to reduce his progress to a walk, the worries began to sluice away as he came to the realisation that he had evaded yet another attempt on his life. The path was narrow here, but he recalled from the hunt that it opened out within the mile and he forced his way through. Low hung branches plucked at the sleeve of his tunic, pulling him this way and that as he rode — a bough caught him a stinging blow in the gloom. His breeches had ridden up and thorns and brambles scored the young duke's calves as the horse shouldered them aside, but high above the star studded sky was a belt of light pointing unerringly towards safety and he pressed on.

Soon the worst of the obstacles were behind him, and with the drop in pace came the opportunity to take stock of his situation. The duke's mind filtered the options available to him as the horse plodded on. He had hunted these lands only the previous day and many times before, he knew them well, and as the sickle moon came into view above to light the way he reached his decision. The castle of his loyal servant Hubert de Ryes lay not more than a dozen miles ahead. The track joined the road from Valognes to the town of Carentan which guarded the crossing point of the River Vire. Cross the river and the duke knew for certain that he was back in the lands loyal to his rule, but he may need help to get that far and Hubert was the father of three fine sons, each knighted by William's own hand. It was the perfect destination, and with the moonlight painting the woodland with its steely light and the path widening the duke put back his heels and risked a gallop.

He made good time, and as the night sky began to pale and the stars lost their lustre, William left the track and regained the main thoroughfare. The first smear of grey on the eastern horizon told of the nearness of the new day as he cantered the final mile, and soon the crenelated battlement on the keep of Castle Ryes hove into view atop its sheer sided motte. The first flicker of dawn was lighting the sky as duke William rounded the final bend and came to the home of his friend, and soon he was guiding his horse across the draw-bridge and through the barbican into the bailey. A small church stood to one side, and the rhythmic chants of Lauds floated across the courtyard as the duke eased his travel weary body down from the saddle and led the beast across to a water trough. As God fearing as any man in Normandy, Hubert de Ryes was almost certain to be at the service which marked the dawn of the new day, and William made the sign of the cross as he drew back the door and dropped silently onto a pew at the rear. Raising his eyes to scan the benches William was gratified to see that his guess had been correct, the four men of the de Lacey family filling the front row of the tiny space, and he relaxed for the first time since the minstrel Taillifer had caused him to be dragged from his slumber hours before as the words washed over him and he made his own peace with God. Very soon the service was over, and William made the sign of the cross as he regained his feet and slipped back outside. The horse was still there and the duke moved around it, running a practised palm along the fetlocks and shanks, checking the hooves for stones and debris as any good horseman should until a cry of surprise told him that de Ryes had exited the chapel. Duke William raised his eyes, smiling for the first time that day at the looks of astonishment which lit his friend's features as they hurried across. 'I have had a bit of a night,' he quipped as they fussed around him. 'But I am among friends now, and I wish to complete my journey with all haste.'

Hubert de Lacey looked at the duke in astonishment. Barefoot and dishevelled there could only be one explanation. *'Trahison?'*

William nodded. 'I was attacked at Valognes by Grimoult du Plessis acting on behalf of Guy of Brionne.' He shot them all a look, all the humour driven from his features as the men quailed beneath the savagery contained within it. 'I have the names of the leading men and they will be dead or in exile before the end of summer.'

Hubert spoke again. 'May I ask their names lord? It may help me to aid your escape if I know which lands are disloyal.'

Duke William reeled off the names supplied by Taillifer in his bed chamber the night before, and the four men shared a look as the scale of the revolt was laid bare. 'You will need to cross the River Vire lord, and quickly,' Hubert said. 'The easiest way would be to carry on south and leave the Cotentin through the town which gives the region its name....' His voice trailed away, and the palm of a hand beat a tattoo on his thigh as he thought. Finally Hubert shook his head. 'If the revolt is as widespread as you say, the conspirators would have moved to block off that route of escape as a matter of urgency. After all,' he said with a gleam in his eye. 'Their heads depend on it.'

Henry de Ryes put in a suggestion of his own as the elders deliberated. 'I could lead the duke to the ferry at the mouth of the river, father. There are no more bridges downstream, and if the town of Cotentin has fallen to traitorous knights, I expect that the roads and crossing points inland will be guarded.'

The de Ryes men looked to the duke for his reaction: they were not to be disappointed. 'It is a good plan,' William said. 'We leave immediately.'

Henry rushed to arm, and Hubert indicated to his younger sons with a flick if his head. 'Hugh, Ralph — go with your brother while I find something a little more appropriate for the duke to wear.'

By the time the horses were saddled the trio could be seen descending from the keep, and William spooned another mouthful of the porridge which the priest had served up as the villagers gawped from a respectful distance. It was plainer fare than that to which he was accustomed, but warming and hearty after the trials of the night before; it reminded the duke of being on campaign, and the thought cheered him further as he saw in it the sign that his counteroffensive against the traitors had already begun. Clad now in stout riding boots and Hubert's best cloak William was beginning to feel less like a fugitive and more like the duke of Normandy, and he clasped the older man's hand in thanks as he climbed back into the saddle. The de Ryes boys were mounting their steeds on the far side of the bailey, and William turned his face to their father as he hauled the horse's head around to face the gatehouse. 'You have my thanks Hubert, I am in your debt.' He cast a look at his surroundings as the brothers walked the geldings across to join him. A bank, ditch and wooden palisade, the barbican and even the keep itself hewn from the woodland which surrounded them. Perfectly serviceable for a minor lord it had none of the grandeur of his betters, and William pledged to put that right. 'I never forget a friend,' he said earnestly. 'As soon as I see off these renegades, we will see to replacing your wooden walls with the finest *Pierre de Caen,* magnificent Norman limestone.'

William was away before the lord of the manor had time to react to the statement, angling a horse now rejuvenated by a well earned rest and a bellyful of oats over to and through the shadow cast by the barbican on its stout oak posts. The drawbridge thundered beneath the hooves of the knights as the de Ryes brothers slid seamlessly into his wake, and William guided the horse northeastwards as he led the group towards the coast. Soon the River Vire was glimpsed through the trees on the righthand side, the surface shimmering as the sun rose higher, and within the hour they were approaching the place where it emptied into the sea. William reined in as the trees drew back to reveal a wide estuary dotted by sand-banks between rock strewn shorelines. He turned back as his companions came up. 'Where do we cross?'

As the elder brother Henry spoke for them all. 'There is a ferry at the tip of the headland, lord,' he replied. 'We can take the boat and the horses can swim alongside. It's only a short distance, if we hold their reins they will be fine, I have done it many times.'

William nodded. 'Lead on Henry. If it is as easy as you say we shall soon be back in Falaise, and we will see what the king of France has to say about cowardly attacks upon faithful liegemen.' The duke reflected on the brothers as Henry led the group towards the coastal path. It was unusual to find three knights living at the family home and he wondered at it. That he had been negligent towards them was now obvious, all men of note craved land and a hall of their own, but he would ensure that each had ample opportunity to distinguish themselves in the upcoming war and they would reap the rewards of their loyalty.

As Henry de Ryes rounded the final bend the silvery waters of *La Manche* came into view, and William filled his lungs with the invigorating air. Offshore the fishing boats were returning to port after a hard night's work harvesting the deep, the chaos of gulls which squawked overhead testament to the fish gutting onboard as the fishermen raced to become the first to deliver their catch to market. The boat which was to carry them across was clearly visible on the shoreline, and William shared a few words with Hugh and Ralph as their brother negotiated the fee. Within a few moments Henry was beckoning them down to the strand, and the trio dismounted as the ferryman and his helpers began to manhandle the rowboat into the shallows. Men came to unsaddle the horses and soon they were ready to board. 'You sit amidships, lord,' Henry smiled as the duke cocked a leg over the side. 'It is the most comfortable and stable part of the boat.' William was not about to argue. Their ancestors may have been Northmen, but the Norman aristocracy had long since lost their love of the sea along with their barbarous speech and adherence to the creed of Oðinn. Now they were as French their neighbours.

The duke took his place at the widest part of the boat as the saddles were distributed, and the younger de Ryes hauled themselves aboard and took their places in the stern. Willing hands heaved the small craft into deeper water and soon the ferryman was arching his back, oaring the craft upstream as he sought to bring them safely to the far bank. For a while the horses were able to tread the sandy bottom, the beasts creating waves of their own as they bobbed along, but as deeper water was gained and they sank to their withers the killers made their move.

Before William could react a blur of movement marked where a rope had been thrown over his shoulders from behind, and as the duke struggled to free himself he froze as the chill of a sharp blade at his throat told him that his struggles would be in vain. The rope was being tightened as Henry de Ryes left his place in the bow and crouched before him, and William fought down the urge to hawk in the traitor's face as he resolved to die like a duke of Normans. 'We will do you a final service, William,' the knight said as the horrified ferryman leapt overboard and struck out for the shore. 'Even the bastard son of a tanner's daughter deserves better than a death by drowning.' Henry clicked his fingers as if he had just recalled something of little importance. 'Oh…' he added with a look of glee. 'I almost forgot. You would have done well to ride straight to Carentan. A pedlar arrived at the castle just as we rose for church, carrying the startling news that the duke had narrowly escaped an attempt on his life. He told us that Walter de Lacey and the rest of his merry band are holding the bridge in the town, as they anxiously await their lord's arrival.'

The duke watched as Henry de Ryes raised his eyes, clearly exchanging a look of joy with his brothers in the rear of the boat. 'It is an ignoble end, but you are the acknowledged son of old Duke Robert.' A curt nod, and William gasped as he felt a hot gush at his throat and the dagger did its work. 'So we have opened your throat before we tumble you over the side.'

AFTERWORD

Of all the instances where duke William came close to assassination, perhaps the two examples I have chosen to recast above came nearest to success. William inherited the duchy on the death of his father in 1035 when he was seven or eight years old. Robert the Magnificent had died on the way home from pilgrimage to the Holy Land, but before he left he had sworn the nobles of Normandy to support William as heir. In addition the duke arranged for three powerful figures to support his son in the eventuality: Alan of Brittany was to act as guardian, William's uncle Robert archbishop of Rouen brought the church onside all overseen by the power of the French king, Robert's liege lord Henry I. This triumvirate appears to have kept the ambitions of the Norman aristocracy in check for the first few years of William's rule, but with the death of the duke of Brittany in 1040 the storm broke.

Orderic Vitalis tells that the young duke was often hidden in the homes of peasants in order to survive capture or assassination, and a succession of guardians died in quick order. Gilbert of Brionne and Turchetil were murdered within months of each other and Osbern Seneschal, Osbern the

Steward in English, was soon added to their number. It seems that the young William really was kept for safety within Osbern's bedchamber in the castle at Le Vaudreuil, and that he witnessed his would-be assassins get close enough to cut his guardian's throat before he was rescued by the timely arrival of loyal forces. William would later repay the debt he owed the family by rewarding the seneschal's son, William FitzOsbern, with the earldom of Hereford following his loyal support both in Normandy and England during the conquest.

The early 1040s must have been a time of enormous danger for the young duke, but he was growing and maturing under the ongoing protection of the church and king of France. With every passing year he continued to forge close friendships with the young sons of his guardians and supporters, the nucleus of the army which would follow him to England in 1066. Matters came to a head in 1046/7 with the plot to replace William with his cousin, Count Guy of Brionne. Whether William travelled to the castle at Valognes to hunt as in our second tale or to face down the rebels is unclear, different chroniclers favour one or the other, but it does appear that the duke was warned by a minstrel that he was in imminent danger and forced to flee in his nightwear to save his life. The young duke made it by way of backwoods tracks to the castle of the minor noble Hubert de Ryes, where the count sent his three sons to escort William to safety in Falaise rather than murdering him as in our tale. You can still walk a small section of their journey today, from Asnelles to the River Gronde, along the pathway known as *la sente au Bátard* — the Bastard's path. Back in lands loyal to him the duke raced on to meet with the king of France at the town of Poissy near Paris, where William reminded the king that an attack on a loyal underling must be seen as an attack upon the French king himself. Henry agreed, and in 1047 rode west at the head of an army in support. That their combined host was outnumbered 2 to 1 tells of the scale of the threat, but when the forces met in battle at Val-ès-Dunes the insurgents were put to flight with heavy loss.

Remarkably it was the first time that duke William had fought in a pitched battle, and he was not to do so again until the very first time he would lead a field army in battle as sole commander — facing an English shield wall on a Sussex ridge almost twenty years later.

6

SPEAR HAVOC

London - 10 October 1066

The king settled back, his gaze slipping from face to face as his closest companions exchanged grimly determined looks. 'I shall run through the plan one last time to ensure there is no room for any doubt. If there are any questions, now would be a good time to ask.' He sketched a weary smile. For a man well into his fourth decade the exertions of the last month had begun to take their toll. Harold took a sip of ale, his mind at last beginning to relax a little now that all had been decided.

This had been a day of comings and goings as men had continued to arrive in the city from all across the kingdom. The king like any good commander had sought out trusted men, tallying the numbers and encouraging them to share their thoughts. Harold glanced towards the window as he replaced the cup on the table before him; it was growing late and he felt as if he had been talking all day. 'We organise the men into their divisions tonight and get as much rest as we are able. When the bells toll for the third hour we leave the city and begin our march to the coast, that will give us time to break our fast and include any latecomers in our plans.' Harold's eyes focused on his younger brothers at the far end of the table. Little more than a week had passed since their brother Tostig had fallen facing them in battle, and he valued their loyalty above all others. 'Gyrth and Leofwine will add the men of their earldoms to those of London burh and accompany me first to Rochester and thence south through Andredes Weald to the coast. By my reckoning that will give us almost eight thousand spears, roughly the same number as our opponents, but we shall have the advantage of fighting on ground of our own choosing and I have just the place in mind.'

Harold's gaze switched to take in the men seated at either side of the long table. Kinsmen now through his recent marriage to their sister Eadgyth, Harold allowed himself a moment of self-congratulation as he looked on the faces of the northern earls. With a family stake now in the success of his kingship, they had already displayed loyalty and fortitude in the fighting against Harald of Norway and his invading army in the recent fighting around York. With the kingdom now united under his rule, nothing but an act of God could carry the day for the Norman invaders. He smiled again. 'Edwin and Morcar, it pleases me greatly to see you among us after all you have endured over the past month, but the numbers who followed you south are understandably reduced through losses and distance. It would be asking too much to expect them to fight again in the spear havoc of the frontline after so short a time, so I was gratified you thought it no slight to your honour when I asked that they be added to the levy men of the southern shires.' The king's features softened as he added a quip, and the men sat about him took heart to see their leader in such a fine mood. 'Also, it would upset the southern folk if the Angles of the North kept all the glory for themselves.' As the gentle laughter receded, Harold continued with his summary. 'The fyrdmen of eastern Kent and those from Surrey will muster at the hamlet of Edenbridge on the old Roman way which marks the border between their lands. The remainder, those from Sussex, Hampshire, Wiltshire and Somerset near the coast at Lewes. Detach a strong force to sweep the coastal towns and villages for enemy foragers, invest the newly built castle at Pevensey where Norman keels first touched English land, and drive the invaders back to the new camp outside Hastings. The overnight stop at Edenbridge will cost a further day's march before you reach us at the hoary apple tree,' Harold said, 'but that cannot be helped. Besides,' he said with a look. 'These are my own ancestral lands and I know them as well as any man alive. I myself witnessed the duke's cautious nature not more than two summers ago, when he withdrew his army from before the town of Dol the moment his supplies came under threat. William has blundered again; hemmed in by the River Brede to the north and the treacherous tidal reaches of Pevensey Bay to the south he thought to have made his position unassailable, but they have only served to trap him with his back to the sea and only the single road out.'

Harold's eyes moved on, settling on the slightest figure at the table. 'Edgar,' he said, pinning the young ætheling with a look. 'You will remain here in London for two more days along with archbishop Stigant. Men are still coming in from all across the country, and I would have you bring them to Rochester and onwards to my army in the south. I have William penned in and I mean to keep him there. I witnessed just how deadly their mounted knights could be on open ground when I fought alongside them in Brittany, and it's not a thing I wish to see repeated in my own land.'

Harold charged his cup, the men seated before him copying the gesture as the king drew the strands of the plan together and prepared a final toast to their success. 'So myself, Leofwine and Gyrth will add the thegns and fyrdmen of London and the East to our housecarls and cut the only road out of the peninsula at dusk on the thirteenth. By the following evening the northern earls will have joined me with their own housecarls and the bulk of the Wessex fyrd, and Edgar and the lord archbishop will arrive with the last of the men who had made it to London the day after that. Their arrival should enable us to give the men in the front line a well earned rest. The year is winding down quickly now, this late in autumn it will take William the best part of the morning to strike camp and advance the half dozen miles from his base in Hastings to the ridge I have it in mind to defend.' Harold smiled his wolf smile. 'By this time next week the air of France shall be filled with piteous laments, and we shall be raising our own voices in thanks to God for this year of stunning victories.'

THE EARL of Mercia urged his horse to the crest of the hillock and drew rein. To his surprise the town of Lewes was not so different to those in the North: hummocky hills, the slopes thickly wooded, with only the brilliant chalk of the summits and scars which peeked through here and there contrasting with the more muted shades of Pennine limestone to show that he was far from home. Below him the army was at last beginning to form up in their battles ready for the march, and he let his mind wander as flashes of colour showed where war flags unfurled in the light autumn airs.

The journey south had been a casual affair, and he acknowledged the king's foresight. Although they would never admit to such, especially in front of southerners, the men of Northumbria and Mercia were all but spent after the hard fighting against Hardrada's Norwegians the previous month and the frantic march south.

But a few days rest in London had worked wonders on war weary minds and bodies, and their spirits had soared as they were cheered through the city and across the great bridge to the burh of Southwark. Following the old Roman road known as Watling Street for the first few miles, they had left king Harald's army near the sleepy hamlet of Peckham and picked up another of ancient Rome's greatest gifts to the North, the road now known as the Lewes Way. An easy day's ride had brought them to the first assembly point, the town of Edenbridge where the earls of Mercia and Northumbria had spent an agreeable night entertaining the thegns of Kent and Surrey, getting to know the names and assessing the qualities of men they could expect to be fighting alongside in the coming days. Slowed down now by the men of the fyrd the twelfth day of October had been an even more leisurely affair than the day which had preceded it, but the weather had been fine, a watery sun and light breeze filling the air with a golden rain as the russet canopy of the great woodland of Andredes began to shed its leaves in preparation for the winter which was fast approaching.

The sound of hoofbeats drawing near interrupted the meanderings of his mind, and an instinctive smile lit his features as Morcar came up. The earl of Northumbria called out as the horse slowed to a walk. 'We are all set brother, and I have come to bid you godspeed.'

The pair clasped arms as Edwin gave a cheery reply. 'May the Almighty also ride with you Morcar, one more battle and the kingdom is secure.' Down in the vale the harsh call of a battle horn summoned the last of the stragglers to their duty. Edwin and Morcar edged their mounts across, taking in the army with a sweep of their eyes as the sound was picked up on the breeze and carried away to the East. 'You have the larger force,' Edwin said, 'and the tougher task ahead. But I watched the men of the western shires last evening as they guzzled cider and belted out their songs, and pity the Bastard and his invaders if they should ever get to meet.'

With a final nod to his sibling Morcar hauled at the reins, guiding the head of his mount back towards the roadway and the waiting column. Edwin watched his younger brother go. Yet another of the myriad roads the Romans had left in this part of the world led directly along the Downs, seventeen miles from Lewes to Pevensey and the wooden castle which the invaders had begun to construct the moment they set foot on English soil. An unfamiliar mix of Northumbrian housecarls and the West Saxon fyrdmen of Hampshire, Wiltshire and Somerset were heading their way that morning bent on destruction, and he would lead the men of Kent, Surrey and Sussex itself along the ancient track which led directly to the king's army twenty-five miles distant. Edwin glanced upwards as the tramp of booted feet reached his ears from the roadway. The sky was a vault of blue, the ground as dry as old bones: good marching weather. The timing was perfect. They would reach Harold's army at the hoary apple tree just before dusk, attack the Bastard together and crush his proud neck.

EDWIN DIPPED his head as another bough reached out across the track, exchanging a look of exasperation with his closest hearth man as the path ahead showed no sign of widening.

Wulfmær glanced across and smiled. 'I have seen wider badger runs lord.'

The earl snorted at his housecarl's jest. Dressed for war the man shone like a newly struck coin in the gloomy surroundings, and Edgar was about to reply with a comment of his own when he saw the man stiffen. Years of hunting down Welsh raiders in country just like this had honed the big man's senses, and the earl drew rein as he too cocked an ear to listen. Riders were approaching, the speed of their advance betraying the importance of their task.

Wulfmær spoke again. 'We would have heard if the scouts had run into trouble, lord.' He cast a contemptuous look at the trees which surrounded the column. 'The sound of fighting would have carried, even in this.'

Edwin drew his sword from its scabbard as the thud of hoofbeats on the earthy ground grew in his ears. At the head of the army where any good leader should be, the width of the track would preclude any help from those following on if this was a Norman war party. But any attackers would be faced with the same conditions, and he had full faith in the man at his side and the deadly axe which had already appeared in his hand. They would fight their way through, hoping that the track widened out up ahead so that the rest of his hearth troop could come forward to help the pair finish the job. The rider when he appeared was clearly English, the rufous beard and shoulder length hair confirmation enough, and Edwin relaxed a touch as he recognised the man following on as one of the Sussex men who had gone ahead. The horseman skewed to a halt before the earl and lost no time in fulfilling his errand. 'King Harold asks that you come on with all speed, lord,' he blurted out. 'The enemy reached the king's position not long after dawn, and the first assault was made within the hour.'

Edwin nodded that he understood as he pumped the man for more details. 'You witnessed the attack?'

The rider bobbed his head. 'Yes, lord.'

'And it appeared to have been carried out by duke William's army, it is not just the chance meeting with a strong detachment, foragers or the like?'

The rider nodded again. 'The Bretons are deployed on the left flank, the Flemings and French the right: duke William and his Normans hold the centre. There is no doubt lord,' he said earnestly. 'The enemy banners are in full view and the numbers tally with our reckoning of their full strength.'

The Mercian earl cursed. They had barely travelled half a dozen miles that morning and the majority of that had been on the well made road which led from Lewes to Pevensey. 'How far away are we?'

King Harold's man blinked and it was obvious that he had been dreading the question. Edwin sympathised. It was all but impossible to catch a glimpse of the sun in the thick press of trees, thereby marking the passage of time and by that estimate the distance travelled, but he needed to know. Thankfully the South Saxon scout had been listening in and used his greater local knowledge to supply the answer. 'We are still about twenty miles shy of the fight, lord,' he said. Edwin's gaze switched to the man as his mind began to plan his response. 'Does the track widen out further on?'

The scout pulled a face. 'In places lord, but never more than enough to allow three or four horsemen to ride abreast.'

Edwin clicked his tongue as he thought. It was late morning, and despite the urgency of his task it must have taken the rider a good three hours to reach him here. If an experienced messenger dressed for speed on a fresh mount had needed that length of time to reach him, the heavily armed horsemen to his rear must take four to make the return journey. He looked back at the local scout as he came to a decision. 'Ride with our friend here and overtake the earl of Northumbria and his army. Tell my brother all that has happened.' Edwin snorted, drawing questioning looks from the men before him as he searched for a way to word his message in such a way that he could be sure his younger brother would act upon it. Morcar was cocksure, a perfect quality for an earl of the independently minded northerners, but it sometimes had its disadvantages. 'Tell my brother that I strongly suggest he abandon the attack on the castle at Pevensey and hurry north to come upon the enemy from the rear.' Edwin fished inside the purse at his belt. 'Here, show him this token — my brother will recognise it instantly and it will confirm your message is genuine.' He smiled despite the tension in the faces surrounding him. 'There will be more than enough ways to die today, without being put to death as a suspected spy. I will lead my own housecarls and the thegns and mounted men of the south-east to the battlefield, with those on foot following on as fast as they are able.'

His orders given Edwin smiled as he came to realise that he would be fighting that day after all. 'The king has proven time and time again that he is a battle winner. He was confident that he could keep the enemy penned in with the Londoners and the men of the eastern shires alone, and I share that confidence. Let the invaders exhaust themselves in futile attacks, and we shall arrive in good time to drive them into the sea.'

THE MERCIAN FELT a hollowness twist his gut as he ran his eyes across the distant ridge line. Half a mile to the east mounted knights were cascading down the slope, driving the tattered remnants of the king's army before them like a fox before hounds. At his side Wulfmær swallowed hard as he formed his thoughts into words. 'The standards are taken,' he croaked, the distress he felt at the sight causing his voice to quiver.

Edwin looked, and knew the king was dead. Even at a distance the earl could see the golden wyvern of Wessex being tossed from lance to lance. No fighting man, particularly his brother-in-law, would abandon the ancient symbol of the West Saxons and leave the field of battle alive. As the clamour of the victorious Norman army rent the cool air of an English autumn, Wulfmær gripped his lord's sleeve and exclaimed in wonder. 'Look!' he said, pointing. 'There are men still fighting!' Near the northern end of the ridge a host of Englishmen stood back to back beneath the triple seax flag of Essex, the dying rays of the sun flashing from sword, axe and spear blade as they sold their lives dearly like the heroes of old. The sight cleared the fog of indecision from the earl's mind, and he searched about for a place to make a stand as the first of the fleeing army plunged into the woodland to his left.

Nearby the fading light picked out a hollow in the earth flanked by a series of ditches, and his eyes flicked to the rapidly approaching Normans and back as he gauged its value as a makeshift defensive work. The underbrush was thick, waist high grasses shielding the drop from the horsemen bearing down upon them, and Edwin knew that Merciful God had at last favoured an Englishman that day. Hauling the head of his mount around he pointed out the ridges and gullies, raising his voice to carry above the jangle of bit and mail shirt as the horse thegns of southern England began to spill from the woodland path. *'Gather there! Form a line!'*

Guiding his own mount across he snatched a last look across his shoulder. The pursuing Normans were now little more than a hundred yards distant but he was at the lip of the drop in a trice, and Edwin's hand closed about the handle of his shield as his feet touched the earth. He raised his voice again as men slid from saddles the length of the ditch. 'Every third man hold the horses, the rest of you prepare to fight. We are too few to carry the day, but we shall give them a bloody nose and then retreat back the way we came.' Edwin's voice became a snarl. 'Make as much noise as you can. Let's see if Normans can fly.'

As the shield wall formed and the staccato beat made by spear shaft and sword pommel resounded in the dusk, Edwin saw the moment when the horsemen became aware of the new threat. He mistook the leading rider for an Englishman for an instant, the man's magnificent flowing moustache flashing gold in the dying light, but the cheeks of those surrounding him were clean shaven and a quick look at the gonfalon, the distinctive banners of the invaders, confirmed that they were about to fight Eustace, the Count of Boulogne, one of the Bastard's most important allies. The count pointed with his lance, and Edwin's eyes flashed with joy as he watched the horsemen wheel away from the fleeing fyrdmen of Harold's army and gallop in his direction. 'Keep up the noise lads,' he called as the thunder of hooves grew in his ears. 'Don't give them a moment to think.'

The leading element was little more than a dozen yards away when Eustace spotted the danger before him and began to rein in, and Edwin cursed his luck as he prepared to order the men alongside him to remount for the fight. But the mass of riders following on were unsighted, and despite the frantic attempts by the leading men to order a halt they ploughed into the rear, forcing the count and his bodyguards over the lip and down into the first of the ditches. Unaware of the danger ahead and eager to add a final chapter to the glorious tale of the day the men of Boulogne came on, and the waiting English watched gleefully as the look of triumph on the faces of the riders was replaced by disbelief and terror as the turf disappeared beneath them and they crashed to the ground. At his side Edwin was aware of Wulfmær fingering the haft of his war axe, the big housecarl straining like a leashed hound to get among those who had brought death to so many of his countrymen; a snatched glance along the line of shields showed that the rest of his men were struggling to keep their discipline as the shield wall edged back and forth like a lapping sea. But English self-restraint held, and the Mercian earl waited until the last of the riders had come to grief before filling his lungs to hurl the ancient war cry of the English into the dusk:

Ut!-Ut!-Ut!... Out!-Out!-Out!...

The chant was taken up all along the line, and a moment later Edwin was leading a landslide of Englishmen down the bank and into the witches brew of broken bodies and flailing limbs filling the depression. Edwin raised his sword as he ran, his eyes flicking from side to side as he searched for the count. To his disappointment Eustace had disappeared from view in the scrum, but a knight was just rising to his feet as his mount kicked and whinnied before him, and Edwin leapt the belly of the horse as his sword blade scythed the air to lay open the enemy's neck just above his mail shirt. As the man crumpled, the sound of broken and panicked horses was swamped by the shouts and cries of the men of southern England as they too fell upon the men from Boulogne. Wulfmær had moved ahead, his axe blade a blur as Edwin's leading man waded into the fray, heads and limbs flying around him as he gathered a deadly harvest.

As the English fighters slammed into the invaders the tide of war momentarily left him isolated, and without an opponent to hand Edwin ran his eyes around the bowl of the depression. The dip was filled with English thegns and housecarls, axe, sword and spear blades reddening as they drove all before them, and Wulfmær backed to his lord's side as the English crossed the floor of the gulley and began to hack their way up the opposite slope. The disordered resistance was fading quickly as the survivors of the rout abandoned their broken horses and streamed away, and Edwin searched their number for the man he wanted to kill before he too managed to withdraw from the trap.

A knot of swordsmen had already regained the relative safety beyond the ditches, and Edwin's heart sank as he recognised the figure of the count harden from the ruck. Guarded by a screen of knights Eustace was already hauling himself into the saddle of a commandeered horse, and the English earl cast about for a spear as his quarry threw back his heels and the horse began to move. At his side Wulfmær had guessed his intent, and he let the Dane axe drop to the ground to snatch a hand axe from his belt. The pair exchanged a look, and Edwin's eyes widened with renewed hope as he snapped out an order: *'Yes! Do it!'*

The housecarl drew back his arm, and an instant later the pair were willing the axe towards its target as it spun end over end through the air. Both men thrilled to the sight as they watched the axe fly true, but God it seemed still had a liking for the enemy that day as they saw the spin of the weapon bring the poll of the axe head and not the deadly blade around to strike Eustace between the shoulder blades. The count lurched forward as his retainers moved in to hustle him to safety and Edwin thought to pursue them, but Wulfmær's hand was already picking at his sleeve as he indicated the field beyond. Hundreds of knights had left the field of death and were galloping down towards them beneath the lion flag of Normandy. It had to be duke William himself, and Edwin knew he was staring at a battle he could not win. 'Back!' he yelled as the last of the Boulonnais fell to avenging English blades. 'Back to the horses! We have given them something to think about, it is time to save ourselves and prepare to fight again.'

EARL EDWIN ARCHED his back and let out a sigh. It had been a long night of chilled air and stone cold food as they had waited patiently for the moon to light the way ahead, but it peeked above the trees in the southern sky now and it was finally time to get the army moving. It seemed like an age since he had parted with his brother on the sun blushed knoll outside Lewes but in reality it was less than a day, and he hoped that the messengers detailing the disaster and the tale of his own fight had got through.

The retreating horsemen had reunited with the men on foot a little over five miles from the place where they had defeated count Eustace and his knights. The heavy cloak of nighttime had been drawn across southern England by then, and Edwin had ordered all brands extinguished as he explained to the leading men what had occurred since they had parted. He had left scouts to watch the enemy from cover, good men who knew what was at stake and could be trusted to act with caution, but he hoped and believed that the chances of an enemy made bone-weary by a full day of battle pursuing them into the inky blackness were slim. To have moved forward to confront the army of King Harold in the early hours of the day meant that the Normans must have been forewarned. Edwin suspected that they had been stood to arms for the entirety of the night, before marching out to take on the English host at first light. Now, with the moon risen to light their way, the time had arrived for the men of Kent, Sussex and Surrey to move forward to renew the assault on duke William's exhausted men.

Within the hour the path began to open out as the track neared the hollow where they had routed the men from Boulogne, and earl Edwin raised an arm in the agreed signal that the horsemen should dismount. Gathering up his weapons from their carrying places he watched as the horses were led away, and the thegns and housecarls who would form the front ranks in the coming fight moved forward to take their places in the battle line. The moon had moved on in its celestial wanderings, the steely light of the early hours reduced to little more than a ghostly bloom as the new day approached, and Edwin cast a quick look skyward as he sent a prayer to God that he should rule that the English had now suffered enough for their sins. The returning light showed that the sky was clear, and as the stars paled only the silvery glimmer which men called the morning star remained visible in the heavens. Edwin exchanged a look with Wulfmær at his side as both men recognised that the conditions were perfect. Dawn itself was almost upon them, and the earl's mind wandered despite the tension of the moment as he led the warriors through the trees. They had hunted a glorious stag in the Welsh Marches for a full day before they had run it to ground in a small copse. Trapped and exhausted the animal had accepted its fate, emerging from the woodland in a flurry of snorting fury as the westering sun painted its horns the colour of blood. The magnificence of the sight had stayed with him to this day, and Edwin hoped that his plan would have the same effect on the battle weary men camped on the ridge line half a mile to the East.

Despite the gloom and clinging undergrowth the heavily armed men who would form the front ranks were soon in position, and as the last of the fyrdmen crowded in their wake sunlight flared on the ridge top opposite. Edwin drew his sword, and the sound of steel sliding free from scabbards was repeated all along the line as the leading men followed his action. The earl raised his head as they did so, his eyes reckoning enemy numbers as the returning light bathed the hilltop camp. The first men were moving about, thin lines of smoke rising into the Sussex sky as the cooks and other non combatants began to prepare the first meal of the day amid a charnel house of the dead. Edwin strained to listen as the last of the men shuffled into line, hoping desperately that the messenger he had sent the night before had got through. Eastwards the pinkish hue was growing by the moment, he would have to order the advance very soon whether help arrived in time or not if his attack was to stand any chance of success. But then it came, and he felt the hairs on the back of his neck lift along with the mood of those around him as the distant sound of English war horns hung in the still air.

In the darkness at the woodland edge Wulfmær broke the silence, his words heavy with pride: *'they made it!'*

The pair, earl and housecarl, exchanged a smile. A mile to the South, the Pevensey road must be choked with the army of Morcar and the Wessex shires as they bore down on the foreigners who had thought to invade their land.

Edwin raised his sword arm as he took the first step forward, and the fringe of Andredes Weald reverberated with the answering cry of their own war horns. A heartbeat later he had led them clear of the tree line, and a quick look to either side confirmed that the sight was all that he had wished for. As the mournful cry filled the air the returning sun broke free of the ridge line — spear points blazed, mail and helms reddened in the dawn, and he allowed himself a grim smile as he imagined the disbelief of men clambering bleary eyed from tents to gape in horror as a spectral army hardened from the shadows. Fifty paces and he paused just long enough to ensure that the fyrdmen had left cover, the armoured ranks of the men flanking him setting up a deafening beat as they clashed spear and sword on shield rim and set up their battle cries.

Silhouetted at the crest of the ridge the Normans and their allies could be seen running to and fro, throwing on war shirts and snatching up weapons nicked and blunted by the previous day's hard fighting as the senior men cobbled together a makeshift defence.

Edwin Ælfgarson, Earl of Mercia, strode clear from the battle line. As he did so, the war chants and battle cries of an avenging army died away and the earl revelled in the power of the moment. For an instant he felt the world still as it awaited his words, and Edwin knew then that this was the high point of his allotted span on God's earth. But there was no time to wallow in self regard, his king lay hacked into meat not half a mile away surrounded by an army of the dead: their ghosts demanded vengeance. As the sound of Morcar's approaching host grew louder in their ears Edwin filled his lungs, led the army in three *hurrahs* and broke into a run.

AFTERWORD

Having defeated Harald Hardrada of Norway on the 25 September outside York, Harold of England likely spent the following few days negotiating the surrender terms of the Norwegian survivors with sixteen year old Olaf, Hardrada's son, and celebrating the victory in the city. The citizens of York had readily submitted to the Norwegians following Edwin and Morcar's defeat at Fulford less than a week earlier, and no doubt Harold Godwinson wished to visibly remind them that he was their anointed king. King Harold was still in the city when news reached him of the Norman landing in the South, probably on the first or second day of October. Harold was back in London by the sixth, so he must have discharged the army who had fought so well at Stamford Bridge and raced south with the mounted elite: the house-carls, thegns, and the men sent by his kinsman King Sweyn Estridsson of Denmark.

Unfortunately we do not know for sure who accompanied the king to York, but it would seem unlikely that after all the preparations of the summer the Norman threat would have been completely disregarded at so critical a time. Someone must have been left in charge in the South in the king's absence, and there were plenty of possibilities within the Godwin family itself. Harold's mother Gytha was still politically active and was a major source of support in her grandsons attempts to regain the English throne after the loss of her sons in the battles of 1066. Harold's sister Eadgyth was of course the widow of the late King Edward the Confessor and must have been well known to any man of rank.

A man known only as Wace writing in the eleventh century describes a scene in his *Roman de Rou,* whereby Harold's brother Gyrth attempts to persuade Harold on his return from the north to remain in London to build up his forces, while Gyrth himself leads the initial confrontation with the duke's army. Both Gyrth and Leofwine Godwinson held earldoms in the South, so either would be a natural choice to watch the channel coast while the king was away. If something like this *had* occurred the time available to re-muster the army expands from the few days following Harold's return to London to a couple of weeks, making it entirely possible that the men of the western shires could have reassembled within striking distance of the invader. The town of Lewes would have been the ideal place to gather, located where Roman roads from Wessex and London meet a day's march from the enemy camp.

The fight which we now know as the Malfosse Incident could then take on a whole new meaning. No longer is it the desperate last stand of a defeated host, but the first strike of a relief army. William of Jumieges in the Deeds of the Dukes of the Normans written shortly after the battle itself briefly mentions: 'The long grass hid from the Normans an ancient bank where the Normans were suddenly thrown with their horses, killing one another as they fell suddenly and without warning, one on top of the other.' The twelfth century Chronicle of Battle Abbey was the first to name the incident as the Malfosse, the Evil Ditch, and pinpoint its location as Oak Wood Ghyll, just beyond Caldbeck Hill where the Hoary Apple Tree itself stood, and describe it thus: '… a final disaster was revealed to all. Lamentable, just where the fighting was going on, and stretching for a considerable distance, an immense ditch yawned. It may have been a natural cleft in the earth or perhaps it had been hollowed out by storms. But in this waste ground it was overgrown with brambles and thistles, and could hardly be seen in time; and it swallowed great numbers, especially of Normans in pursuit of the English.' The sources are confused as to the details of the incident, but I have chosen to follow the writings of William of Poitiers who has the attack led by Eustace of Boulogne who, upon fleeing the unexpected counterstrike was struck between the shoulder blades, blood spurting from his nose and mouth just as William arrived with reinforcements. The same writer says there were 'battalions' of men, making use of 'a deep gully and a series of ditches,' and it seems that Duke William also entertained the thought that the position was defended by fresh troops, newly arrived at the battlefield.

The earls of Mercia and Northumbria were certainly in London soon after the Battle of Hastings, sounding out their own chances for the vacant throne. Rebuffed they threw their support behind the young Edgar ætheling before shepherding their sister, Harold Godwinson's queen Edith the Fair, to safety in far-off Chester. If they *had* followed Harold south with their own thegns and housecarls and joined with the men of the southern and western shires as in our tale, the likelihood is that a Norman army already weakened by a day long fight would have stood little chance against them.

7

PEACE WEAVER

Panting like a coonhound, the shaggy haired youth hooked a finger behind the neckband of his tee and gave a tug: 'dude, it's sweltering!'

Karl rolled his eyes, lacing his reply with just enough sarcasm that he hoped his friend would get the message without taking offence. 'In June? Who would have thought?' He was unsuccessful.

'Still, it's the last one for me — you?'

Karl gave a shrug as he searched for an excuse to move off: Ed was far too bubbly a character for moments like this. It was hotter than a pharaoh's sandal and he was about to sit an exam in an airless gymnasium, but he was a good mate and he deserved a reply. 'I have a chemistry paper this Friday and then that's my lot.' Ed's lips began to move just as Karl's eyes alighted on salvation. 'I am parched,' he croaked as he began to drift away, 'best of luck in your final exam, you lucky sod!'

Snaking through the crowd Karl was soon at the faucet, cursing beneath his breath as he bent his head and thumbed the button. Why anybody would choose to plug the hole with gum was beyond his comprehension, but he could almost feel the eyes upon him — willing him to shy away — and he let the tepid, minty tasting stream play across his lips as he affected an unconcerned air despite the churning in his guts.

Thankfully the sound of the double doors opening soon came to his rescue, and as the crowd shuffled away Karl followed on into the school gym and searched the rows for his candidate number. The sunlight streaming in from the windows set high in the south wall neatly divided the room into light and relative shade, but lady luck had had her fun that day and he slipped into a chair in the darkest part of the hall. He took a last look around as he began to compose himself, sparing a sympathetic thought for those who would have to contend with the torch-like glare of the midsummer sun. As the invigilator revelled in his fleeting moment of importance, addressing the packed rows like a drill sergeant on parade, Karl placed the clear bag containing his pen and a spare — black ink only! — in plain sight as instructed.

A waft of perfume mixed with the smell of burnished parquet, a sickly addition in a room imbued with the odour of decades of sweaty armpits and worse, and the paper was on the desk before him. Karl felt his cares melt away as the earlier jitters vanished; history was his thing, and he found that he was looking forward to it after all the years of study.

The hand on the oversized clock behind its protective mesh flicked silently upright: it was ten o'clock exactly and the instruction came to begin. Turning the paper over Karl pushed down the desire to gallop ahead, carefully filling in his name and number as his eyes took in the heading:

THE NEW JORVIK REGIONAL EXAMINATIONS BOARD

For the General Certificate of Education

June Examination 2019 - Advanced Level
HISTORY
Second Syllabus - From Empire to Commonwealth and the growth of the English Speaking Peoples
Two Hours and Thirty Minutes Allowed
Answer ONE question from section a) (60 marks) and any TWO questions from section b) (twenty marks each)

A quick double-check that he had entered his candidate number correctly and Karl opened the booklet, running his eyes down the page as he looked for the question which would supply the majority of his marks. His mind sifted them into possibles, probables and definitely nots as he read. All the stock questions were there: Athelstan the Conqueror's death and the retreat from the East; the effect of global cooling in the mini ice age on the Atlantic trading routes and the differing fortunes in the English colonies of Greenland and Iceland. He was about to sigh inwardly at the predictability of it all when the final question seemed to leap at him from the page, and he reread it again as he reached for his pen and began to sketch out a draft:

The main turning points in the development of the English Empire are generally well known: the invasion and incorporation of the kingdom of France within the empire in response to the anti Huguenot pogroms of 1685; Athelstan the Conqueror's plague death outside Moscow in 1352....

Karl snorted as he read the old exam standard again, his eyes flicking from side to side as he realised that the sound had reverberated around the hall. Heads were turned his way — at the front of the hall Sergeant Rock was shooting daggers. A light thump on the chest and a sickly smile, and he covered up his indiscretion with a cough in the time honoured way before moving down to read the final line of the question:

> *In your opinion are there any other times, perhaps less well known, that the history of England and wider Scandinavia in general could have taken a far different course?*

Karl arranged his papers and mind. This was heaven sent. He had been reading about an obscure period in history only the previous week which was the perfect response to the exam question before him, and he finished jotting down the main points, drew a line through his workings and began….

MOST PEOPLE ARE aware of the Danish conquest of England in 1016, but few realise just how close the kingdom came to a take-over, both clandestine and militarily, by the powerful duchy of Normandy in the middle years of that century.

Following the deaths of Cnut the Great's sons, Harold I and Harthacnut in 1040 and 1042 respectively, a half forgotten son of the line of Cerdic, Edward, was recalled from exile in Normandy to take up the English throne. Supported by the warlord Godwin, earl of Wessex, the early years of Edward's reign were largely uneventful, but as the earl aged and the king's confidence grew England slowly but surely became riven into two opposing camps which could be loosely termed Anglo-Norman and Anglo-Danish.

Edward the Confessor was a son of the English king Æthelræd II *unrœd* and Emma of Normandy, and he invited increasing numbers of Normans to cross the channel to become his advisors.

Godwin had been elevated by king Cnut and was a trusted

advisor of that king. Married to Gytha, the daughter of an important Danish chieftain named Thorkil Sprakling, it seems certain that Godwin would have fought alongside many of the current Danish nobility as a young man and his sons were undoubtably Anglo-Danish.

The first hints of the coming discord between king and earl came in 1047, little more than five years into Edward's reign. The king of Denmark Sweyn Estridsson, a nephew by marriage of earl Godwin, sent a request for aid to the English in his ongoing war with the king of Norwegians. Godwin urged that fifty ships and their crews be sent to aid his kinsman, but the king refused. A few years later Sweyn, now facing the new king of Norway Harald Hardrada again asked for succour, but although Godwin supported his cause king Edward once again turned them down. To make matters worse for the earl, the later years of the 1040s saw increasing numbers of Normans crossing the channel to take up positions of prominence with the king. The most influential of these was Robert of Jumièges, a Norman churchman who Edward had made bishop of London in 1044. There appears to be little doubt that Robert slowly supplanted Godwin as his main advisor, and it seems just as clear that the two men had little time for each other. Godwin opposed the elevation of Robert to the See of Canterbury in 1050, and must have been perplexed when the now vacant bishopric of London was given by Edward to yet another Norman, William, the king's chaplain. The early years of the following decade saw matters come to a head.

The year 1051 witnessed two major events which in my view must be connected. While Godwin and his family were abroad witnessing the marriage of Tostig Godwinson to Judith, the daughter of the count of Flanders, the count of

Boulogne Eustace II was in England meeting with king Edward. Not only were Flanders and Boulogne traditionally hostile neighbours but Eustace had at one time been married to a sister of the English king, and one can only imagine the anti Godwin poison which was dripped into the ear of Edward as he, Robert and Eustace hunted and dined together in the earl's absence. On the return journey the count and his followers stopped outside Dover, donned armour and proceeded to provoke the townsfolk to open hostility. Men died on both sides, and back in the country now Godwin was ordered by the king to lay waste the town as punishment. Dover, as all parties were well aware, was part of Godwin's earldom and he refused to carry out the harrying. Ordered to appear before the king Godwin for once overreacted, mobilising his own forces and those of his sons to confront the Confessor. When the northern earls and the royal housecarls in London declared for the king, Godwin and his sons were forced into exile, exchanging two younger members of the family as surety that they would be allowed to leave unmolested.

With Godwin and his sons seemingly gone for good, Edward was now free to recast the kingdom in the image of an Anglo-Norman continental state. Queen Eadgyth, Godwin's daughter, was packed off to the abbey at Wherwell where yet another sister of the king could keep a good eye on her. Normans were appointed to the vacant earldoms where they began the construction of motte and bailey castles, but most importantly either in late 1051 or early 1052 duke William of Normandy is said to have crossed the channel to England. Sure now that he would remain childless, king Edward apparently bestowed the English succession on the duke as the crowning act of his Normanisation of the country.

But the earl and his sons were not so easily defeated, and by the end of the summer of 1052 they were back in force. Outmanoeuvred, the king was forced to reinstate both the queen and Godwin and his sons to their earldoms. Although Godwin himself died soon after Edward was no warlord, and following the flight of his Norman friends he needed the Godwinsons to help run and defend the kingdom. While Edward lived the situation stabilised, and for the following thirteen years the king seems to have retreated into a life of piety and hunting. During this time the Godwinsons gained influence and power. The eldest son Sweyn had died on pilgrimage, but Harold became earl of Wessex on the death of his father and in 1055 the third brother Tostig became earl of Northumbria. With the later accession to the earldoms of East Anglia and Middlesex by the younger brothers Gyrth and Leofwine, all but the earldom of Mercia in the west were in Godwinson hands.

Perhaps lulled into complacency by the near hegemony of the family and the passage of time, the next flashpoint occurred in 1064. Whether by accident or design, earl Harold took ship and ended up by various means at the court of duke William, where after a summer of campaigning with the Norman leader he asked for the return of the family hostages from 1052. William agreed to release one of them to Harold, his nephew Hacon, on the understanding that he swear on holy relics to support the duke's claim to the English crown when Edward died. Unable to see any other way out, Harold appears to have agreed and returned home with the young man who was now in his late teens, leaving behind his brother Wulfnoth who William promised to deliver up as soon as he became king.

Soon after he returned to England, in February 1065, King Edward the Confessor died and Harold was now trapped by his vow. As earl of Wessex, a proven war leader and the eldest surviving son of Godwin, Harold was in a powerful position to stake a claim for the throne itself, but it was clear now that this would invite an invasion by the powerful Norman duchy and its allies. An assembly which became known to history as the Great Witan of Winchester was called for March 1065. This "meeting of the wise" convened to discuss not only the succession, but the English response to any belligerent moves made by William and his supporters. The Norman duke had already sent emissaries to both the witan and directly to earl Harold demanding that they honour king Edward's settlement and their oaths of support respectively, with a thinly veiled threat that he was willing to come and take the crown himself if it was not forthcoming, and it was at this point that an unlikely champion arose.

Tostig Godwinson's ten year incumbency as earl of Northumbria had been only a qualified success. A southerner, he was already at a disadvantage in an earldom which prided itself in its semi independence from the rule of the kings in Winchester and London at that time. A potent mix of Angle, Dane, Norse and Briton the region had been part of England for little more than a century, and they not only hankered to be led by one of their own but resented the taxes which travelled south. Tostig had responded by riding roughshod over these sensitivities, bypassing the northern lords completely and employing Danish housecarls to collect taxes and administer his rulings. The king of Alba Malcolm Canmore was a close friend, and Tostig's failure to deal adequately with border raids and deeper incursions led to much resentment. The earl even resorted to murdering political opponents, so it was somewhat of a surprise to many when Tostig proposed a solution which would ultimately lead to the byname by which he is known today — Peace Weaver.

A son of the house of Cerdic — the dynasty of the West Saxons — had been brought back to the country several years before from Hungary where he had been fathered in exile by a half-brother of the Confessor. Known as Edgar the ætheling the boy was still only fourteen years old in 1065, but as a grandson of Æthelræd II *unrœd* he had a direct and irrefutable claim to the English throne, and Tostig became the driving force behind the plan to introduce a regency to the kingdom. A similar situation existed at the time in France, where the young king Philip I had ascended the throne on the death of his father in 1060. In that case the regency was being shared between the king's mother Anne of Kiev and Tostig's brother-in-law Baldwin V, count of Flanders.

Edgar was crowned in Winchester cathedral on 14 March 1065, and with the country now firmly united in its support for the new king, Tostig travelled to Flanders leaving the boy in the capable care of his brother Harold. What followed was a masterpiece of statesmanship, unrivalled in England up to that point. Eager to support his kinsman and make life as difficult as possible for his rivals in Boulogne and Normandy the count quickly recognised Edgar as king of the English, and by early summer he had used his influence as regent to persuade the French to also recognise the legitimacy of Edgar's rule.

By that time Tostig had moved on to Denmark, the kingdom ruled by another of his kinsmen, his great-nephew Sweyn Estridsson. Here the earl faced a more difficult task. Sweyn had not only been born in England, he had a strong claim to the crown through his mother, Estrið. This well-bred woman was a daughter of king Sweyn Forkbeard and therefore a sister of Cnut the Great, king of Denmark, England and Norway. As described above, Tostig's father Godwin had urged king Edward to send significant military aid to the

Danes in their ongoing wars with the Norwegian king Harald Hardrada on at least two occasions, and he was finally able to use the goodwill which this generated to conclude a pact of mutual assistance in June 1065: by the terms of this treaty England and Denmark agreed to regard an attack upon either kingdom as an attack upon their own. It was, we can now recognise, another small step which would lead to the permanent merging of the crowns in the following century.

Duke William was now surrounded by what contemporaries called the Ring of Steel, and when Conan II of Brittany recognised king Edgar and his entreaties to the Pope were rebuffed that August, the pretender was forced to stop work on the construction of his invasion fleet and disperse the army.

Could the Normans and their allies have succeeded had they launched their invasion? The methods of warfare used in the Scandinavian north and the European mainland could hardly have been more different. Large scale all-or-nothing battles, whether fought on foot or at sea were still the norm among the northern nations. William could have expected to face overwhelming numbers soon after landing on the English coast. To counteract this he would have undoubtably brought along hundreds or even thousands of workmen who would be put to work immediately constructing the type of motte and bailey castles which were used to dominate the surrounding area. Continental leaders very rarely sought open battle unless the odds were heavily stacked in their favour, the comparatively small size of their domains and the number of potential enemies within a short march of their heartlands gave little chance to recover from a heavy defeat, even if the leaders survived the rout. Earl Harold had already experienced this first-hand the year before when he had campaigned alongside the duke in Brittany. It was warfare based on mounted reconnaissance and siegecraft, and the castle building activities along the Welsh border by Normans brought in during the brief exile of the Godwin clan in 1051-52 only serve to support this. Even if the invaders could have got ashore, formed a bridgehead and constructed these fortifications, the land area of England was simply too vast for this creeping type of conquest to succeed. With the certainty that the Anglo-Danish fleet would deny the Normans any hope of reinforcement or resupply and the likelihood that his own duchy would suffer invasion from France and Brittany in his absence, even a man as obstinate as William was forced to concede that his chances of gaining the English crown were vanishingly small.

So the succession crisis of 1065 became a footnote in history, and England remained not only a part of the Scandinavian north but the engine behind the creation of an empire which would stretch from Novgorod to the Pacific coast of Vinland. One can only speculate what would have occurred had duke William been successful in his quest. With the vast monetary and manpower wealth of the English State now orientated southwards, perhaps the Normans would have swallowed up all the petty kingdoms which now comprise the Commonwealth of France? At the very least centuries of warfare would follow as the armies fought for control of her riches. Deprived of English leadership and treasure, the Scandinavian nations might very well have remained independent but much reduced in influence. Maybe New Jorvik and even Vinland itself would have become Spanish possessions, and I should be writing these words elsewhere?

KARL RAISED HIS HEAD, flicking a look up at the clock on the wall. An hour — pretty much spot on: that left him ninety minutes to answer the following two questions. The sunlight had moved across the floor of the hall as he had written, and he watched in amusement as the invigilator attempted to squint at the scribblers for any sign of cheating. Ed had noticed too, and the friends exchanged a look of amusement as they went back to work.

AFTERWORD

The only detail I needed to tweak to construct this alternate timeline was to move the death of King Edward of England back little more than a year — and it could have been even less — from January 1066 to the previous February. By doing so the greatest impediment to the unity of the English kingdom at this critical time was removed. Tostig Godwinson's character and actions in Northumbria were as outlined above, and the North was driven to revolt. On the 3 October 1065 the Northumbrian thegns descended on York with their hearth warriors, killed Tostig's housecarls and other officials and declared the earl an outlaw. Moving south they were confronted by Harold Godwinson who, sent by king Edward and sensing the depth of their anger, recommended that his brother be stripped of the office of earl.

In hindsight it was the moment that the hitherto unbreakable bond between the sons of Godwin was shattered, and the kingdom was riven by division at the worst possible moment. A favourite of both the Confessor and his queen, Tostig's sister Eadgyth, it appears that the forced banishment of his favoured earl contributed to the death of the king only three months later. With the imminent threat of invasion hanging over the kingdom, the young Edgar ætheling was passed over for the crown and the experienced warlord Harold Godwinson became king on Edward's death; but the kingship was now the proverbial 'poisoned chalice' as he inherited a kingdom torn asunder by the events of the past few months.

Tostig, instead of acting in the interests of the country as in our tale, embarked on a tour of Europe by which he sought aid in reclaiming his lost earldom and revenge for what he obviously regarded as his brother's betrayal. It led directly to the invasion of Harald Hardrada and his Norwegians in September 1066, King Harold's ride north and the battles at Fulford and Stamford Bridge. Harold of England was victorious in the second battle, but it was a hard fight against a formidable foe which in all likelihood cost him victory on a windy ridge outside Hastings a few weeks later.

Everything else in our tale is historical fact, every familial relationship, event or war. It is a sobering thought that something as innocuous as moving the death of a single man, albeit a king, forward by even a few months can drastically change the world in which we live almost a thousand years later.

8

STRANGE CATCH!

The sea fizzed as it passed down the flanks of the longship and fanned out in its wake. Æthelric rested a hand against the tall stern post, filling his lungs as he cast a look outboard — unlike most Englishmen who saw the watery wastes as little more than a roadway for Vikings and invading armies he loved the sea. Astern the other ships in the fleet bounded the swell, their chequered sails taut and full as the following wind drove them eastwards.

Clearing the bone-white nib of Beachy Head, the thegn braced as the ship master heaved on the big side rudder and pointed the prow towards deeper water. The currents were treacherous around the headland, and any steersman worth his salt would do well to give them a wide berth. He had seen the skeletal frames of ships which had been driven aground and knew them for the killers of men that they were, despite their beauty.

The *Brimwulf* was leading the first fifty ships ahead of the main fleet. Tonight they would sup ale in Dover burh, and on the morrow shoot the channel known as the Wantsum before continuing on up the River Thames to London.

The thegn of Kelvedon in Essex, he was looking forward to spending the season of crop gathering and Christmas at home. A summer spent in the south while they waited for the Norman fleet to appear had been, despite the glorious weather, a monotonous round of training sessions and bouts as the thegns and housecarls strove to keep thousands of men fed and occupied. As the month of August had slipped inexorably into September the king had decided that it was too late in the year for the enemy to mount his attack. The season of storms was almost upon them, and with the supplies all but exhausted the men of the fyrd were becoming increasingly worried about the harvest. Satisfied that the threat had faded, king Harold had ordered the army stood down and was drawing his forces back from the coast.

The helmsman spoke at his side as a tidal surge lifted the hull. 'Do you recall the signal for the sighting of the Norman fleet, lord?'

Dragged back from his reverie, Æthelric turned his eyes on the shipman and gave a snort. 'I am hardly likely to forget after a summer spent staring out to sea — I have been seeing red flags in my sleep!'

Eldred nodded, but something in his expression caused the ship thegn's stomach to lurch. 'Yes, lord — a red flag flown at the mast head.' He turned his head to starboard and indicated mid channel. 'A bit like that one, I would guess.'

Æthelric shaded his eyes with the ledge of a hand and peered away to the south. The ship was still hull down on the horizon but the mast was in clear sight, and his mind raced as he saw the blood red signal flag clearly against the greyness of the sky beyond. Fully manned a fleet of fifty ships would have been a powerful force, but they were short handed and hardly in a position to attack the entire Norman fleet. The best warriors, the thegns and housecarls, had returned to their halls and estates throughout the shires and hundreds of southern and eastern England, leaving skeleton crews to sail the ships back to their winter quarters on the Thames, Stour, Yare and others. But they were here, the signal had been seen, and it was clear where his duty lay. 'Steer a course to intercept,' he said. 'Let us see what our countrymen have to say.'

Eldred hauled the steering oar into his chest, and as the prow of the ship began to come about Æthelric snapped out an order to a nearby crewman. 'Repeat the signal from the mast top. Let us make sure that the rest of the fleet know why we are changing course.'

As the vessels converged it soon became clear that the warning flag was being flown by a small fishing boat from one of the many settlements scattered along the English shore, and within the hour the fishermen were drawing alongside the sleek warship. Æthelric watched as Eldred's crew spilled the wind from the sail, taking the way off the ship as the master of the little sailboat gripped the sheer strake and hailed them across the waves.

'The Normans are out, lord!' he yelled. 'They are moving what must be their entire fleet north along the coast.'

It was the news he had expected to hear, but the final confirmation had Æthelric's heart beating a little faster as he stepped forward to pump the man for more. 'How many ships are in the fleet? Where are they headed?'

The fisherman snorted and puffed out his cheeks before replying. 'That's two very different questions, lord — one easy, the other not so much. When we saw them the leading ships were shadowing the coastline as they clawed their way north, but the tail stretched back to the estuary of the River Somme.' He shrugged and pulled a face. 'As to numbers there was a cloud of sail.' He scratched at several days' worth of stubble as he thought. 'There could be up to a thousand I would guess, I could barely see the coastline beyond to north or south.'

Æthelric chewed on his lower lip as he calculated the odds against him. Each of his fifty ships carried ten *butse-carls,* shipborne housecarls, tough, full time warriors. But the ships were sailing under half-crews, twenty per ship. All told he had roughly fifteen hundred men at his disposal, and a quick calculation based on the information supplied by the fisherman came up with the discouraging thought that they could be outnumbered by as many as forty or fifty to one. The thegn was aware that every man on both ships was staring intently as they awaited his decision, and his mind raced. They were daunting odds, and the king would not thank him if he lost a good part of his fleet in a single engagement. Tostig, the king's brother, had already raided the coast that summer and there were rumours that he was in the northern kingdoms, trying to whip up support for further attacks. Æthelric hopped onto the steering platform, shielding his eyes against the glare of the afternoon sun as he peered westwards. More English ships had cleared the headland and were heading out to sea, but the look had told him that the fleet resembled a long ribbon of sails stretching back as far as the Wight.

The leading ships under his command had come up and were wallowing in a crescent around them, riding the waves like gulls in the swell. They would prove a hefty punch if not the knockout blow which the full fleet could bring to bear, and Æthelric wrestled with his decision. With the ships short crewed it was pointless to wait for the rest of them to catch up, and even if they put in to shore to gather reinforcements the army had already dispersed, but he must act decisively or the chance may be lost. Strung out the Norman fleet would be vulnerable to a quick attack — besides they had no great reputation as seafarers, despite their Norse roots. He turned back to the helmsman. 'Eldred, you know the coastline opposite and the tides thereabouts. Do they mean to attempt the crossing today?'

The shipmaster's gaze wandered across to the East as his mind pictured the far shore. Finally he gave a shake of his head. 'It sounds like they are heading towards Cape Grey Nose, the chalk cliffs past Boulogne. They can ride at anchor there for the night and cross the Straits tomorrow without losing sight of land.' He nodded as he warmed to the idea. 'It makes sense, lord. A fleet like that, heavily laden and with inexperienced crews will move at walking pace. They will need a full day to cross, even with a fair wind.'

Æthelric clapped the man on the shoulder as his words confirmed the direction of his own thoughts. Dipping a hand into the purse at his belt, he took out a pouch of silver coins and tossed it across to the delighted fisherman. 'That is to replace your ruined catch. Sail towards the rest of our ships and tell them what you have told me. Let them know that I am heading towards the Straits and to follow on as fast as they can.' The decision made a weight lifted from his shoulders, and the thegn threw the skipper a parting smile as the little boat eased away from the longship and its crew reset the sail. 'I have a bigger fish to net.'

The man laughed and waved as the vessels drew apart: 'strange catch!'

Æthelric turned back and addressed the expectant crew. 'You all heard that. We have a chance to hurt them before they even reach our coast, we must take it. Our duty is clear — we attack!'

. . .

'Look, there it is again.'

Æthelric eased himself alongside the watchman, raising a hand to grip the forestay as he stared out into the darkness. The world was as dark as slate, with only the luminescent flicker of the breaking waves to indicate the junction between the cool air and the colder waters beneath. The English thegn squinted and concentrated where the man had indicated, but still he could see nothing. He was about to suggest that the lookout may have been mistaken when the sea fell away as the *Brimwulf* crested a wave. A point of light winked in the distance before disappearing as the ship nosed down into the next trough, and he made a suggestion as Eldred came up to see. 'A star?'

The ship master shook his head and sniffed. 'Unlikely lord, I have barely seen one all week.'

Æthelric nodded in agreement, it had been a foolish suggestion but he was at a loss to think what it could be. 'Could it more fishermen?'

Eldred shook his head in the gloom. 'Not at this time of the year. They sometimes fish at night in the winter when the waters are colder — cod appear hereabouts and herring shoal, but not until November.'

'A warning beacon on land then?'

The steersman looked back at Æthelric, and the thegn could see the man's teeth shine dully as he smiled. 'Doesn't look like one, lord. If you ask me, I would say that we have found at least one of them.'

Away to the East the first signs of the dawn washed the horizon ash grey, dulling the mysterious light a little more with each passing moment. As the men dressed and armed for battle, Æthelric ordered the sails lowered and the masts of the English ships unstepped and stowed amidships to lower their profile. Every moment they remained unobserved carried them a pace nearer, and with the wind against them but the current running in their favour the rowers conserved their strength, easing the ship southeastward as the steady flow swept them down to what they were sure now was the enemy.

They had hugged the coast of Sussex, making good time as they sped northwards the previous evening. Æthelric knew the sight of a flock of English sail on the horizon would send the Norman fleet scurrying for the shelter of the beaches and harbours of William's ally the count of Boulogne, so he had used the following wind to race ahead. As the white cliffs near Dover came up on the larboard beam Eldred had led the ships out into the Straits, fanning out into a skirmish line as they backtracked in search of their prey. Dusk had found them in mid Channel, and he had drawn the ships of the flotilla together until they were within hailing distance. Now, as the light of the new day approached and the upper works of a magnificent longship came into view he called on them to close up again. If the fisherman from the day before had run his errand the remainder of the English fleet would be following on somewhere out there in the dark, but even half-crewed fifty ships' companies stiffened by butsecarls should be enough to give this Norman upstart a fright.

As they drew closer and the sun finally broke free of the earth the hull of the enemy longship came into full view, and a buzz of excitement ran through the crew of the *Brimwulf* as it became clear that this was no ordinary vessel. The ship was large, surely too large to be anything other than that of the duke himself, and as the butsecarls gathered in the bow and prepared to lead the attack Æthelric drank in the beauty of her form. The hull of the ship was painted in alternating lines of blue and yellow from the sheer strake to the waterline, while above it a sail of matching colours had been shortened the night before as the ship held her station and waited for the rest of the fleet to come up. The fact that this must be the foremost vessel only served to reinforce the ship thegn's hopes that they had found the enemy leader, and as the returning sun clipped the horizon a flash of gold at the mast top set English hearts racing. A brace of flags flew there, the lions of Normandy billowing in a brisk southerly: but it was the flag which revealed itself a moment later which confirmed that they were bearing down upon the duke himself. A golden cross on an ivory field the colours shone as they caught the light, and Æthelric turned to the steersman at his side and fixed him with a look. 'That is the papal banner, the one our spies have reported the duke has been parading before his army to steady the waverers.' He made a fist, slamming it into a palm as he fought to remain calm. 'It would appear that God Almighty disagrees with the judgement of his representative on earth, and has delivered the pretender into our hands.' His eyes flashed, revealing the excitement within. 'Lay me alongside steersman, and we shall do His work.'

As Eldred trotted off to do his duty Æthelric returned his gaze to the ship ahead. To his amazement there was still no sign of life aboard the Norman vessel, and as the sun climbed higher and the visibility improved he saw to his surprise that the ship appeared to be completely alone.

The thegn's bemusement only lasted a moment before he realised with a jolt what must have occurred during the night. Eager to take advantage of the prevailing wind following a summer spent penned within the rivers and estuaries of his homeland, the duke's ship had raced ahead. Naturally he would be sailing the finest vessel on the seas and the others had struggled to keep up. *That* was why the ship flew a beacon at its mast, to regroup, and *that* was why they had still not been spotted by the crew who would be scanning the southern horizon, anxiously searching for the rest of the fleet as the daylight revealed their plight.

Lower in the water with their masts unstepped and to the west of the Norman ship, Æthelric realised that his own ships would appear as indistinct shadows in the gloom, and he urged the rowers on with a sweep of his arm as he strove to close the gap as quickly as possible.

With a last look around the ship thegn unhooked his battle helm from its carrying strap at his side, easing the cold steel onto his head as the first sign of movement appeared ahead. A Norman crewman was scampering up the mast, fighting his way past the billowing flag to extinguish the now redundant lamp in a hiss of steam, and Æthelric watched for the moment when he would cast a look their way. A heartbeat later it came, and the Englishmen aboard the *Brimwulf* laughed aloud when they saw the slack jawed panic of their enemy as he set eyes upon the English ships for the first time.

They were close enough now to hear the seaman's desperate cry of alarm, and Æthelric hefted his shield and spear as he moved forward into the bows and prepared to lead the butsecarls over the side.

A line of faces appeared along the wale on the enemy ship, the horror in their expressions turning to shock as an arrow flew in to punch the first to fall that morning backwards onto the deck, and as another volley drove the Normans back Eldred laid the *Brimwulf* alongside with an expert sweep of the big paddle blade. The moment that English oak grazed Norman the ship thegn was over the side, forcing his way past the line of shields which lined the flanks to land on the decking with a crash. Even before he had recovered his balance Æthelric's shield was sweeping around to cover his head and body, and as the rest of his men thundered onto the deck to either side he risked the first glance towards the stern. With the sail shortened he had a clear view aft, and he forced down his disappointment at the sight which met his eyes as he began to move forward into the attack. Out beyond the sternpost the horizon was now a-brawl with sail as the remainder of the invasion fleet took advantage of a following wind to close with their leader, and Æthelric realised that if he was to gain the victory which was so vital for his nation he would have to move fast. His best troops were with him, the butsecarls already fanning out across the deck as they sought fighting room to swing their deadly axes, and Æthelric broke into a trot as he attempted to close with the enemy before they could organise a defence in depth.

A dozen Normans had already formed themselves into a line amidships, and lifting his gaze the Englishman could see scores more donning helms and snatching up weapons and shields as he rapidly closed on them. Within a few paces he was throwing a shoulder into the back of his shield as he reached the Norman shield wall, and an instant later they met in a bone jarring crash which rocked him back on his feet. Æthelric drove forward, jabbing his spear back and forth as he sought an opening, but the wallowing deck sapped his momentum and the Normans stood firm. A spear blade glanced off the shoulder of his mail shirt, and Æthelric dropped the point of his own, stabbing downwards as he searched in desperation for the breakthrough with would carry him closer to the duke. Within moments he was rewarded as he felt the point of the blade slide into flesh, and as the man before him began to stumble a powerful push into the rear of his shield sent the Norman sprawling to the deck. Æthelric stepped smartly into the gap, finishing off his opponent with a spear thrust to the throat before he could recover. Leaving the spear in the gore the ship thegn moved the hand across to draw his sword, but even as he rejoiced in his victory the sight which met his eyes caused him to check his stride.

The Normans had recovered quickly from their surprise, and little more than a spear's length before him a solid wall of mail clad knights barred the way. A helmeted head flew across his line of vision and he knew that the butsecarls had finished off the rest of the advanced guard, and as the thegn wormed his way between the deadly barbs and brought his sword crashing down on the steel dome of a helmet, a thunderclap of noise told him that the axemen were already battering the shields to either side.

Æthelric peered above the rim of the shield as he raised his sword arm to stab at enemy faces, his eye line the only vulnerable spot between the steel of his helm and the mail coif which protected his head and neck; but even as he looked he began to despair at the quality of the men who now stood in ranks between the men of the *Brimwulf* and the man they must kill. The distinctive slurp of an axe blade pulled from flesh reminded him to withdraw his head, and as the follow-up strike hissed by inches from his face Æthelric took a backwards pace and then another to give the shield wreckers more room to work.

Beyond the reach of Norman spears for now the Essex thegn threw a look to either side as he sought to judge how well the fight was going. Off the larboard beam another English ship was about to disgorge a host of fighters, but like his own they consisted mostly of shipmen with a handful of butsecarls, no match for the battle hardened knights who crammed every inch between the mast and the figure of the duke near the stern. He took another rearwards pace, lifting his chin to peer out beyond the gilt cherub which graced the stern post of the duke's ship, and a knot of fear tightened in his guts at the sight which greeted his eyes. The Norman fleet, a line of sail on the horizon only a short while before now smothered the sea, the bow waves sparkling in the morning sunlight as they pounded north to rescue their lord. Seeing the approaching danger the rest of the English ships were moving to come between them — but the wind was gusting in their faces, and with no time to step their masts they were creeping southward under oar power alone.

The first of the newcomers from the English ship had reached his side now, and despite their desperate straits Æthelric sketched a weary smile as he saw that they were led by his old friend Skapti Egilsson from the *Thurrock.* As that ship's butsecarls rushed forward to support those from the *Brimwulf,* Skapti shook his head. 'We are not going to make it,' he cried above the roar of battle. 'The Norman ships will sail around our lads and leave those following on to finish them off.' He plucked at Æthelric's sleeve. 'Order the men back to the ships, we have done all we can. Carry the news of the invasion back to the king in London, and he can set about recalling the army and march to defend the coast.'

Æthelric looked back towards the fighting. Despite the reinforcements the butsecarls were making no headway against the packed defence, and it must be as clear to Norman eyes as English that they just had to hold their formation and the fight would soon be won. Æthelric was about to bow to the inevitable when an idea came to him, and he moved his head closer as he yelled above the din. 'Get the crewmen back aboard the ships, and then form the butsecarls into a defensive arc around the place where you boarded.' Skapti's eyes widened in surprise, but before he could open his mouth to speak Æthelric snapped again. 'Do it quickly, and we may still have a chance.'

As Skapti moved off Æthelric began to flick the wooden decking up away. Every ship leaked water, even those newly constructed for an invading duke, so the wooden decking had to be made removable to give easy access to the waters sloshing about in the bilges below. This time however the Englishman had the very opposite in mind to baling. As the first boards came away the sour smell of green oak wafted up from below, and the thegn shook his head as he saw just how newly cut the wood used to build the ship really was. It was true he reflected as he stepped down into the dirty brown water lapping the keelson, the Normans really had forgotten their Viking roots. Streaked by tanning, the oak strakes which clad the hull already looked to be straining against the nails which fixed them to the ribs, but the roar of victory in a foreign tongue drew his gaze away as the order to retreat passed like wildfire among the crewmen and they fled the fighting. Æthelric watched as the butsecarls moved shoulder to shoulder, drawing swords and short seax for the coming close order work as they shuffled back towards his position.

The sight of the fleeing seamen was too much for Norman discipline, and the front ranks broke free to skewer and hack at any head or back they could reach. As he had hoped the thrill of the chase overtook the Norman knights and most veered left to attack the crew of the *Brimwulf* rather than face the grimmer prospect of confronting the still formidable looking block of butsecarls, and Æthelric cupped a hand to his mouth as he called out to two of his own. 'Oslac! Wulfric!' Recognising his voice above the din the pair turned his way, and Æthelric indicated that they join him with a jerk of his head. 'More axe work,' he yelled as they stepped down into the bilges. 'Hack out as much as you can between each rib.' As Oslac and Wulfric set to, Æthelric reached out to grab an axe from the deck. Several of the butsecarls had already fallen that morning but there was still more than enough to put up a fight, and he took comfort in the fact as he started to believe that his ploy would succeed.

Æthelric gripped the haft and swung, thrilling to the sight as the very first stroke sent a chock of the soft green oak spinning away. As he raised the axe to swing again Oslac was crying out that he was through, and the thegn shouted a reply as his axe chewed another wedge from the hull. 'Keep going — we need to scuttle her before help can arrive!'

The Norman knights had finally realised the danger, and Æthelric snatched a glance as they renewed their assault on the butsecarls whose heels now teetered on the very edge of the drop. He pushed the picture from his mind as he swung again and again, and within moments he was rewarded by a sudden surge of seawater. The water level was rising fast, the depth of it now drawing the power from the strike, and Æthelric spun around to hack at the side strakes as the longship began to settle. Before he was through the vessel gave a lurch, and as he was thrown to one side Æthelric thrilled to the sight of a great upwelling of seawater cascading onto the deck. As the angle steepened and knight and butsecarl alike began to slide down the slope, Æthelric leapt up to the deck and looked outboard. The closest Norman ships were still half a mile away to the south with the English flotilla snapping at their heels like angry hounds, and switching his gaze back to the stern he saw that the tightly packed defence was now a chaotic brawl as seaman, knight and duke alike tumbled past the mast. Æthelric bellowed a command as the duke's ship dipped her bows into the waves and seawater poured across the wales. 'Save yourselves lads, back to the *Thurrock!*'

A quick thinking crewman there had tossed a rope across

to the nearest butsecarl, and Æthelric made a grab for his belt as the planking of the deck began to shift beneath their feet. The Englishmen formed a chain with the hafts of their axes as they began to scramble over the sheer strake of the *Thurrock* to safety, pausing only to stab dagger and seax blade into the faces of those Normans who tried to cling to them in their own desperation. As he was hauled aboard Æthelric rolled onto his back, staring in wonder as the hull of the enemy ship rose to the vertical and began to slip beneath the waves. Perched at the highest point now the golden cherub which graced the stern post now resembled a weather vane, and as the Essex thegn scrambled to his feet and the last of his men were dragged aboard, they watched in awe as the magnificent vessel pirouetted beneath the heavenly messenger before disappearing beneath the surface in a vaporous pall.

A shocked silence had descended on the men of the *Thurrock* now that their enemy had gone, but Æthelric was already on his feet, his eyes searching the waters for any sign of duke William. Weighed down by their armour the knights and men at arms were already on their way to the bottom, but the Norman crewmen were clinging to flotsam and there was no room for mercy in his heart that day. Twenty yards away, beyond the men now struggling in the water, the crewmen on his own ship *Brimwulf* were walking her mast upright as the need to escape Norman vengeance overtook any feelings of pity for men about to die; Æthelric called out for the seamen on the *Thurrock* to do the same as bowmen lined the wales to finish off the Norman survivors. Away to the South the other English ships were beginning to detach themselves from the fight as they too saw the fate of the duke's ship, stepping masts and setting sails as they turned their bows for home.

Caught up in the enormity of the moment the hand that rested on his shoulder gave him a start, but he turned to see the smiling face of Skapti Egilsson and scoffed at the words which followed. 'You have a famous victory Earl Æthelric.'

Kelvedon's thegn returned the smile as a dull thud shook the ship, the *Thurrock's* mast slid home, and his friend spoke again. 'Let us go and tell the king that he may not have to recall the army after all.'

AFTERWORD

King Harold stationed the ships of his fleet in the bays and estuaries surrounding the Solent that summer as the army waited for the Normans to appear on the horizon. It was the perfect position for them, easily provisioned and upwind of the most likely landing areas. As summer began to turn to autumn and the invasion threat receded, the king withdrew his ships to their winter berths on the Thames and ordered the seaborne levies of the *scip fyrd* back to their home ports. Had the winds been favourable there is little doubt that the Norman fleet would have sailed earlier than it did, and a naval battle may very well have occurred.

Æthelric of Kelvedon actually existed and gets a mention in the great survey of 1068 commonly known as the Domesday Book. Here he is said to have fought a naval battle against William in the channel, but took ill and died on his return to London leaving his estates to Westminster Abbey.

Duke William's ship *Mora* was a gift from his wife Matilda. It was the largest and finest ship in the invasion force, and I based the description of it from its depiction on the Bayeux Tapestry. This sleek longship's sailing qualities were such that it *did* become detached from the rest of the fleet the night before the landing in Sussex, and a beacon was lit at the masthead to act as an assembly point. Despite this the following morning found the ship and her occupants alone in mid channel, but the English ships had already passed through the Dover Straits and were back in their Thames side berths. Not for the first or last time that autumn, fortune smiled on William.

9

A CRUSHING VICTORY

Lincoln - 23 September 1066

The newcomer wormed his way into the group, drawing a growl and a veiled threat from the nearest man as he held his hands out to the brazier. 'Keep your elbows to yourself friend, or you'll not be in need of a warming.'

King Harold winked at the men opposite, and their expressions lit up with glee as he followed up with another gentle nudge. The man spun around with a snarl, but his voice trailed away and he gaped like a lackwit as he recognised the figure of the king. 'I gave you fair warning — now if you don't….'

The group laughed as their friend's expression became a mask of horror. 'I am sorry lord,' the housecarl stammered. 'I thought you were one of the men.'

Harold grinned and clapped him on the shoulder. 'I rather hoped I was one of the men.' His look encompassed the group as he continued. 'Every man who fights for me in the coming war shall become my brother.' The king watched in satisfaction as a look of pride illuminated each face in the group. He had always had the ability to inspire fighting men by word and deed, and in truth he greatly enjoyed their company. He had felt humbled that they had returned to his banner in such numbers when he had recalled them so soon after their release from duty on the South Coast. Men were joining them each and every hour as he sped north to confront Harald Hardrada's Norwegians and those of his own brother, Tostig. He knew that most of them had barely arrived home when his riders had arrived to ask for their spears and shields once again. The blare of the assembly horn had torn them away from harvest and family, and Harold resolved to reward them all handsomely once the crisis had passed.

The first reports of the attacks in the North had reached London five days previously. The coastal town of Scarborough had been attacked and burned, after the inhabitants offered fierce resistance to the Vikings on their journey towards the mouth of the Humber. The town had sent word to earl Morcar in York, and Harold's brother-in-law had immediately sent a messenger speeding south. The last communication the king had received had told him that the earl's brother, Edwin of Mercia, had summoned his army and was rushing north to join their forces together to resist the invader. Harold had left London on the twentieth and gathered men as he rode the Great North Road. In two more days he would be in the capital of Northumbria and they would see off this challenge together.

A nagging fear tugged at the king's mind. The South had been emptied of its best fighting men and his spies told him that duke William had still not dispersed his fleet nor paid off his army of mercenaries, but there was little he could do. He must go north or risk losing the population there. Many were descended from earlier Scandinavian invaders and their allegiance to the southern kings was not so firmly rooted. It was the reason why he had married Edwin and Morcar's sister early in his reign, so he simply must act decisively.

A clamour drew their attention across to the old Roman gate, and the group looked across as a horseman rode into the square. Despite the gathering gloom the king could see that the rider looked all in, and the lathered flanks and heaving chest of his mount told them all that the horseman had ridden hard to overtake the king. Men were pointing in his direction, and Harold left the fireside as the messenger slid from his saddle and hurried across, pushing down the fear which gripped him at the tale he was about to hear. The worst news he could receive was that the Normans had managed to cross the Channel in the South while he was racing in the opposite direction with the finest troops in the country. If that was the case and he was forced to chase the Norwegians all across the North it would be a disaster. Harold pushed the fears down with difficulty; the chess pieces were in movement and he would have to play the game the best he could. His mind returned from its worrying, and he watched as the horseman hurried across the square. Seeing the king's expression the messenger painted his face with a reassuring smile as he came up and began to deliver his report. 'You have a crushing victory, lord!'

The warrior tore the fastening strap from a leather pouch and fished about inside. As the men nearby began to spread the sensational news, the message-bearer dipped his head and passed a rolled parchment to the king. 'Earl Morcar offers his congratulations and sends this token of your victory, Lord King.' Harold reached out to take the proffered scroll as the messenger drew a dark bundle from his satchel. The king indicated that he unfurl what looked to be a flag as he picked at the wax seal with a thumbnail, and his face lit up in wonder as the banner fell open to reveal the outline of a swart raven in flight. A gaggle of tough housecarls stood close-by, Danes sent by Sweyn Estridsson their king to help his kinsman Harold in this year of dire threats, and the sight drew an audible gasp from them as they recognised the flag and its importance. Harold looked across. 'So, this is what I think it is then?'

The Danes nodded eagerly, the joy they felt at witnessing the sight shining in their eyes. 'Yes, lord. That is Land-waster, the war flag of Hardrada.' They all shared a look. 'Of all the races on God's earth the Danes should know, it has been the bane of our lives since we were bairns.'

Harold nodded as he began to unroll the message, still dazed by the suddenness of it all. The Norwegians and Danes were sworn enemies. Harald Hardrada had come south, raiding the coast of Jutland practically every year during that time in his efforts to deprive the Danes of their independence. As an English thegn pressed a cup of ale onto the grateful messenger, King Harold took himself aside and settled down to read the contents of the scroll by the guttering flame of a nearby brand.

Our King!

Together this day we have met the army of the King of Norway and driven it from your kingdom. Harald the Hard Ruler lies slain and your brother Tostig is in our power. You will be pleased to learn that he is unharmed and awaits your judgement.

Harold rubbed his face wearily as one concern replaced another. He was glad that Tostig had survived, and hoped that they could find a way to live together in peace once this tumultuous year had passed. Perhaps he could bend a little and offer his brother their traditional family power base, the earldom of Wessex, once his position as king was secure. One thing was certain, he was lucky to have been granted quarter by men who had risen against his rule only the previous year. He pushed the thoughts away as he read on with mounting excitement. Tostig was a problem for another day.

Our scouts shadowed the Norwegian fleet as they followed the course of the River Humber before following the River Ouse as far as Ricall. Here they disembarked and hastened forward in battle array. The combined armies of Northumbria and Mercia advanced manfully from the city to Fulford, and here they set their standards. With their flanks secured by the River Ouse and a deep dyke, the English stood firm as the invaders approached and formed their own shield wall.

Battle was joined and almost immediately the men of Mercia under their earl tasted success. Driving forward they swept into and through the forces commanded by your brother and chased them from the field.

Seeing the disaster unfurl on their right flank the Norwegians, resolute beneath their Land-waster banner, Oðinn's bird, that hated symbol of heathendom, wheeled and struck the Mercians in their own flank. Many English died as they were forced into the waters, but the army of Northumbria struck back. As the pressure on them eased the men of Mercia rallied. Crushed between our armies, the Norwegians fell almost to a man.

The king lowered the parchment and looked up to find that a ring of expectant faces had gathered at the edge of the circle of light. He beamed at them as he confirmed all their hopes. 'It is true. The enemy has been routed and chased from the kingdom.' As cheers rent the cool evening air, Harold calmly ran his eyes through the closing paragraph.

The North is safe and stands firmly at your side. We have assembled a force of two hundred housecarls which will ride south to join with your household troops two days hence. A further force of five hundred mounted bowmen from Mercia have already left for the South and should reach London within the week. Together we will ensure that the Norwegian survivors leave our land and stand ready to support you on the South Coast should the need arise. I have sent Hardrada's Land-waster flag to you as symbol of your victory and to strike fear into the Norman host should they dare to invade.

Let the Bastard come, and we shall see him off together!

Your faithful kinsmen,

Edwin, Earl of Mercia

Morcar, Earl of Northumbria.

King Harold rolled the parchment and laughed at the ribald antics of the men before him. He really was happiest among fighting men. Harold snorted as a big housecarl tipped a barrel of ale over himself, shaking his locks as his friends offered up cups to catch the drips.

'Yes…' he breathed as the yips and yaps of exultant men echoed back from the ancient walls. *'Let the Bastard come if he dares.'*

AFTERWORD

King Harold was forced to retire from the South Coast on the 8 September as his supplies ran low and the men of the fyrd agitated to return home to gather in the harvest. The ships of the fleet left their station at the Isle of Wight and returned to their winter berths in the Thames the same day. That very day, far to the north at Tynemouth, the fleets of Harald of Norway and Tostig Godwinson had come together for their joint invasion of England. Moving south, the fleet of up to five hundred longships harried the coast before entering the River Humber and moving on York.

Earl Morcar would have known of the invasion within days of their arrival off the River Tyne. He called on the forces of his brother, Edwin the Earl of Mercia, to come to his aid and sent word to his brother-in-law, the king. It is estimated that Harold knew of the situation by the sixteenth and he set about recalling his army from the shires. Leaving London on the twentieth, the same day that the northern earls fought the battle of Fulford, he moved north, adding to his army as he went. Five days later, after a forced march covering almost two hundred miles, he fell upon the Norwegian army at Stamford Bridge and destroyed it utterly. Within days the Normans had landed in Sussex and the depleted, travel and battle weary English army hurried back south.

But what if the northern earls had won the first of the great battles that autumn of 1066? No war leader leaves the safety of a walled city to give battle unless he is confident of victory, and although outnumbered the northern earls had chosen an excellent defensive position; their combined army should have been able to go toe to toe with the Norwegian invaders, despite Harald the Hard Ruler's formidable reputation. With the Norwegians rebuffed and king Harold still in the South, it would have been far easier to recall the men of the levies who had so recently been stood down from their summer long invasion watch.

The spectacular march north of Harold and his men is a clear indication of the power and organisation of the mid eleventh century English State. Even without reinforcement from the North, most continental observers at the time thought that the odds on an English victory were overwhelming.

10

WALLINGFORD BURH

Late November 1066

A gush of hot urine spattered the roadway and the earl jumped smartly away. Looking up, his mouth widened into a grin as the acrid smell of horse piss filled the air. 'That is enough leg stretching for now,' he quipped. 'It should have cleaned the mud from my boots at least — I want to look my best when I go calling on a duke.' The flow showed no sign of diminishing, and casting a look at the trackway his features became a frown. Every rut, hoof mark and footprint within a half-dozen feet of the steady stream was rapidly filling to the brim, and Waltheof hauled himself back into the saddle before he was forced to paddle across.

Ulfketil Wæcnan flashed him a grin of his own as the earl settled back at his side. 'That's good luck lord, or so my brother always said.'

Waltheof widened his eyes in question as he took up the reins. 'Hereward said that?'

'Aye, lord,' Ulfketil chuckled: 'Hereward the Wæcnan,

terror of Bourne. I cannot wait to see his face when he hears the tale of this night!'

The earl nodded. 'Well, he is the terror of Flanders now I hear. He may harbour strange ideas about what amounts to good fortune, but we could have used his axe this past year.'

The earl's eyes returned to scan the dark ramparts of Wallingford, the burh walls brooding beneath a leaden sky, and Waltheof's mind drifted back across the events which had convulsed the kingdom since the old king had died in January as the torrent of horse piss finally petered out beneath him.

The year had started well. King Edward had gone to God on only the fifth day of the new year, nominating Harold earl of Wessex as his successor in the surefire knowledge that it would trigger an invasion by the king's kinsman William, duke of the Normans. Soon confirmation had reached them that the river banks and shipyards of the duchy were swarming with ship wrights as keels were laid and planking sawn, and as the new king's brother Tostig had harried the coast the northern earls of England had looked on with wolfish intent as all their scheming had begun to bear fruit.

The unexpected invasion of Northumbria and the defeat of Edwin and Morcar by the king of Norway could have proven fatal to their plans, and Waltheof as earl of Huntingdon had seen no option but to join his forces to those of Harold Godwinson as he sped north to chase the invaders from a kingdom he still thought his own. But in a remarkable twist of fate not only had Harold crushed the threat to their heartlands but Tostig had died in the fight alongside his Norwegian ally, and as the plotters had met to celebrate both their deliverance and the death of the man who had been their earl little less than a year before, word had reached them of the duke's landing in the South.

Returning home to reinforce their armies the leaders of

northern England: Edwin of Mercia; Morcar of Northumbria; Oswulf Eadwulfson of Bamburgh and earl Wulfheof himself had bided their time until Harold was forced to move south to confront the threat without them. Within days the northern earls were in London, where they were greeted by the sensational news that Harold along with his brothers the southern earls Gyrth of East Anglia and Leofwine of Middlesex had been slaughtered by the invaders alongside the majority of the Godwinson supporters. It could only be the work of God that a family whose reach and influence had seemed unassailable little more than a year ago could be all but wiped out in so short a space of time. But if the Lord was said by some to be an Englishman, events were to prove that he must be a northerner to boot. As the English fleet had scoured the coast of enemy shipping, trapping the invaders and denying them fresh troops and supplies, the Normans had pressed on. With his army withered by hard fighting and dysentery, duke William had gambled on a decisive thrust towards the capital. Rebuffed at London Bridge, the invaders had been channelled further inland until they had reached the ford at Wallingford in their bid to force a crossing of the River Thames; now they would discover that the walls of the town they had thought to afford them protection were little more than a trap.

Stretching before him the Oxford road ran as straight as any spear shaft towards the northern gate, and Waltheof's eyes fixed upon the portal as he awaited the signal. It must come soon, the dawn even this late in the year was only a short while away, and he was about to utter a curse when he saw the first signs of movement. Within moments the big oak doors were being pulled inward, and the men in the column came alive as they prepared themselves for war. Waltheof flicked a sidelong look at Ulfketil as a dull glow began to flicker on the oaken boards. 'Godspeed old friend,' he said.

'If you can cut the picket lines and drive away the Norman horse, the war will be won within the week.'

The big man nodded, casting a rearward look as his men began to urge their mounts forward. 'We will not let you down, lord. There are no men better suited to horse rustling than fenland folk.'

Waltheof stole a look as his hand moved down to unfasten the ties which held his sword secure in its scabbard, stifling a snort as he saw again the type of men there. Where the Lincolnshire thegn had unearthed a band of cutthroats and ne'er-do-wells from his land of sokemen and wapentakes at such short notice he hadn't a clue, and it was plain that there was not an honest warrior among them. Dressed in the earthy colours of their trade, spears and lashes replaced the showier arms of his own men; but they were just the type for the task ahead, and he sent a word of thanks to God that the Wæcnan clan and their acquaintances were on his side. The earl twisted around further, exchanging a nod with the men who would fight at his side: his own cousin Cospatric, shining like a silver penny alongside his housecarl Swegn; Brand, the leading man in Waltheof's own hearth troop tensed like a bowstring ready to loose.

He looked back towards the town, just in time to see the buttery glow of the torch move into view and the shadowy outlines of signaller and gatehouse harden in its light. As the flames began to arc back and forth, Waltheof clapped Ulfketil on the shoulder and put back his heels.

On the higher ground to the East, the leaders of Northumbria burst into life as the horsemen spilled from the distant tree line. 'Here they come!' Morcar exclaimed. He shot the man at his side a look of joy. 'Now we will see how far these

Normans can get without horses.' Oswulf's lids narrowed as he followed their progress through the murk. As head of the family dominating the old kingdom of Bernicia from its fortress of Bamburgh, he had as much riding on the attack as any man — even the West Saxon wretch Edgar who still thought he would be king of all England. He snorted. Tonight, the southern fetters which had bound them for a century or more would be cast off forever.

Morcar edged his horse forward with a squeeze of his knees. One last look to the South, and he watched as the attackers slid from their saddles and began to run towards the town gate. Sure now that the attack was going to plan, he turned his head aside to call a command. 'Light the fires!'

Sparks flashed as men bent over flints and steel fire starters, and soon the battle line was aglow as brands were carried forward and thrust into pyres. As the flames took hold, Morcar looked on with satisfaction as the flickering light slowly revealed the conquering army of Northumbria. A look to the north and the army of his brother Edwin of Mercia were doing likewise, and as the shield wall emerged from the gloom, the air above the rising ground was filled with the shrill blare of war horns. 'That should grab their attention,' he said as the first battle cries rolled down towards the Thames.

Oswulf turned to Morcar and pulled a lupine grin. 'We shall have to remember to thank the duke for choosing the ideal place to rest up for our attack.'

The earl returned the look. 'I rather doubt that he will get the chance.'

It was true the Bernician reflected as the first flames appeared in the town below, duke William and his ragtag army had been most obliging in choosing to cross the River Thames at this point. Although the main northern armies were already in London when the Normans arrived on the

South Bank and had shadowed them as they moved inland, an army requires far more than arms and armour to fight a prolonged campaign. The burh which had developed into the town of Wallingford had been placed deliberately to guard, not only the crossing place, but the route known as the Icknield Way. Thought by learned men to have been already ancient when Caesar's legions had covered the earth, the Way traversed the high chalk hills of the Chilterns to intersect the later Roman roads of Watling Street and Ermine Street north of London. Along these arteries could flow not only fresh fighting men, but supplies from the Mercian and Northumbrian hinterlands. With the harvest safely gathered food for the men and fodder for horses was abundant, and Oswulf allowed himself a smile; not only could they lay siege for the entirety of that winter if needs be, they could rotate the men in the besieging army to keep them fit and disease free. With Godwinson dead the English leadership had become a hydra: chop off any head and another sprouted in its place.

Morcar interrupted his thoughts as the battle line set up a din. 'It's a shame about the inhabitants.'

Oswulf looked. The fires near the northern gate were taking hold, leaping from rooftop to rooftop as a gusting breeze got up. He sniffed and gave a shrug of indifference. 'Saxons? War and fire are like sausages and mustard — they are both tasty enough, but they are far better together.'

THE WALLS of Wallingford burh rose before him as the horse galloped down the road. Waltheof Siwardson, earl of Huntingdon, hunched his shoulders as he rode, half expecting the searing pain which would accompany the arrival of an arrow from the walkways ahead. When none came he stole a last look away to the west. Ulfketil and his band of ruffians were already more than a hundred yards away, barely visible as a darker mass against the night sky beyond as they swung around to the south. Brand came up blocking his view, the housecarl's eyes already stabbing the defences as his shield came around to protect his lord. Waltheof raised his head; the doors of the burh had been drawn inward as they rode and he could see the first buildings within by the light of the signaller's torch, but he hauled at the reins as he came into the shadow of the walls and skittered to a halt before he passed through the gateway into the small clearing beyond. He was on his feet before the dust had settled, sliding his left hand into the shield grip as he drew his sword with the right, and he set off at a run as the sound of armoured men dropping to the ground filled the air.

His duty fulfilled the torch carrier moved aside, and Waltheof hunkered into his shield as he pounded past him into the town. The earl's head whirled from side to side, his eyes knifing the shadows as Brand and Cospatric arrived at his shoulders, and satisfied that he had not been led into a trap he relaxed a touch as the courtyard filled with his men. His arm shot out, stabbing the tracks and alleyways which led into the heart of the burh, and within moments the groups of heavily armed men were disappearing into their inky blackness. Waltheof stomped across to the man who still held the torch and made a demand: 'who are you?'

'Wigod, lord,' he replied, 'the thegn here.' Before Waltheof could speak again the man was beckoning to the shadows, and the earl spun on a heel as he prepared to defend himself. Wigod cut in as a group of folk appeared from the door of a nearby building and he recognised the danger. 'They are my kin and the other important inhabitants of the town. I persuaded them to remain in the burh until the Normans arrived,' he explained. 'If the invaders had realised that Wallingford was without its leading families they would have suspected that all was not as it seemed.'

Waltheof nodded. 'Get them out of the town and into cover. Your king and the old West Saxon lords have drawn up their army across the western road. I cannot spare you any horses,' he said with an apologetic look towards the women and children gathering by the gatehouse, 'but they are not too far away.' He clapped the thegn on the shoulder as the first shouts of alarm in a foreign tongue carried to the yard. 'Here,' he said, holding out a hand to take the flaming torch. 'Let me have that, and go to your lord.'

Waltheof switched his gaze to the grassy bank enclosing the town, and the parapet and walkway which topped them. He could see that his men had already chased away any opposition, and with his escape route secure he turned back and beckoned Cospatric. 'Kinsman,' he said, offering up the blazing torch. 'Can you get your men to fire the thatch while I see to our defences.' He shot his cousin a smile. 'I suspect that it is about to get much hotter around here in more ways than one!' He turned to find Brand as Cospatric began to bellow his orders, only to find the big housecarl already at his shoulder where any bodyguard should be. 'Let us go and wet our swords and axes,' he said with a scowl. 'As soon as the fires take hold we pull back.' Both men looked up as the first fronds of flame began to show at the eaves of the nearest hall. Near the centre of the town they could see the lion flag of Normandy stretched out to the south, and they shared a look as they realised its importance. 'Well, the rising wind should speed things along — let's get going.'

As Waltheof and his hearth troop pounded along the road which led to the heart of the town, the earl raised his chin to look ahead. He had been in enough burhs, the fortified towns built in the days of king Alfred and his successors, to know that the layout had been standardised; four roads intersected at the centre, each running away to exit at a gateway cut through the enclosing ditch and bank with a palisade and walkway above. He had instructed the leading men to draw up into a defensive position well before the centre was reached, and as the backs of his men appeared barring the roadway ahead he began to check his stride.

A face appeared at a doorway and was quickly pulled back; Waltheof turned aside to kick the door open before it could be slammed shut and barred. Ducking inside his shield swung up and around, and as his sword arm went back and the room resounded to his battle cry he took a pace aside as Brand followed on. In the grips of his war fury it was all that the earl could do to stay his hand as the candlelight revealed the occupants to be a churl and his family, and he spoke quickly as the terrified group shrank back against the wall. 'Are there Normans here?'

The man shook his head and blurted a reply. 'No, lord.'

Waltheof quickly ran his eyes around the room as Brand moved forward to overturn settles and make sure. He could see why. The single roomed hovel was barely big enough for the family, the floor of beaten earth without rushes, the walls bare of any decoration. 'Leave this place,' he growled, 'and get yourselves into the woods as fast as you can. There is an English army outside, they will feed you until you can return.' Without waiting for a reply Waltheof indicated to Brand with a flick of his head, and a moment later they were back on the roadway and closing in on the rear of the English shield wall. Men turned his way as they heard the tramp of booted feet, the wide smiles all-telling as the battle line opened to admit their leader, and Waltheof's heart leapt as he came up and saw the strength of the position they had chosen. A small brook cut the road on its way down to the Thames, its banks now steep sided as the need for more building space within the town walls had taken precedence over the years. What had once been a thing of natural beauty had now become little more than a drainage ditch, and the stench of animal and human waste was cloying despite the chilliness of the November air. Immediately ahead a short wooden bridge carried the main north-south roadway across the watercourse, and mid span the imposing form of Ulf of Torksey stood amid the bloodied corpses of the latest enemies to fall to his axe.

'He has been there since we arrived, lord,' a voice said at his elbow, 'and nowt will cross while he remains.'

Waltheof nodded. He had witnessed Ulf's axe work already that year, when they had chased away Tostig Godwinson and his Vikings from the Humber in the spring and more recently against the same man and his Norwegian friends at Stamford Bridge outside York, and knew the spearman's words were true. On the far side of the channel enemy soldiers were beginning to gather in numbers, but the sight of Ulf and the results of his butchery were enough to dissuade them for the moment.

Safe from attack for now, the earl looked along the bank. English shields stretched away in both directions, and lifting his head he saw Cospatric and his northerners anchoring the line. Their spears were less than he would have liked to defend such a wide position but the trench would form a formidable obstacle, and if the men at his side were lacking in numbers he knew that their qualities and fighting spirit were second to none. The first hint of smoke reached Waltheof's nostrils, and a quick glance across his shoulder showed flames spurting from rooftops beneath a crown of windblown embers as the fires took hold. The counterattack could not be long in coming, and he decided on a change of tactics while they still had time. 'Brand,' he snapped.

'Yes, lord?'

'Send men to tell the battle line to withdraw far enough to let the housecarls swing their axes. Reform the shield wall half a dozen paces from the lip of the ditch, and tell them to be ready to pull back to the main gate when they hear a long falling note on the war horn.' He raised his eyes again before turning back. In the short time that had passed since he last looked the fires had grown, sinuous flames now licking the night sky. He called again, and the giant stopped and turned back. 'Tell them to be ready to repel an attack at any moment. The Normans and their lackeys have awoken to find themselves surrounded by fire, noise and enemies; but they will see us taking up a defensive stance, and they will take heart thinking that our own attack has stalled at the trench.' Brand nodded, hustling away to pass his orders, and Waltheof returned his gaze to the far side of the ditch as the flicker of distant flames to the East reflected from Northumbrian mail, helms and spear points on the hillside. Shouts and curses in French drew his attention back to the south. A member of the Norman nobility, the shaven nape confirmation enough, had arrived and was cajoling the disparate group into some semblance of order. Another attack would be coming, and soon; Waltheof watched as the English line reordered itself and the axemen advanced. Brand was back: Waltheof opened his mouth to speak but the housecarl answered the question before he had time to ask it. 'My place is at your side, lord,' he said. 'We have enough axemen.'

The harsh note of a trumpet call cut the air, and Waltheof turned back just as the Normans gave a cry and burst forward into the attack. Ahead the housecarls began to swing, the cold steel of their blades reflecting the approaching flames as they whirled faster and faster. The first of the enemy were down in the ditch, and Waltheof ran his eyes along the nearside lip as he waited for them to reappear. A line of shields edged into view as the first Norman fighters struggled up the bank, and the English battle line watched gleefully as they were swept away by the death dealing axes. The housecarls took a pace forward, the blades continuing to scythe the air in deadly arcs as they reaped a grisly harvest, but more were appearing by the moment and soon sheer weight of numbers told. As the first Norman spearmen broke through, Waltheof advanced. Off balance the first attempted to throw his shield across to deflect the blow, but the earl's sword was already in motion and Waltheof felt the blade bite through flesh and bone as the Norman's shoulder crumpled. The sword blade came back, Waltheof hacking down onto the head of the spreadeagled enemy as he raised his eyes to pick out the next threat.

To his right a housecarl fell, spitted by a handful of spears like a cornered boar, and as the gap opened up before them the Normans gave a cry of victory and surged forward. But if the momentum was with the attackers the stout hearts of the defenders had their measure, and as English shields crashed together and spear points stabbed out in reply the Norman breakthrough was driven back into the gully.

To the fore another Norman squirmed past the sweep of the housecarl's axe and Waltheof stepped up. But Brand edged past his lord in his eagerness, and the earl was forced to watch as the big man hammered the attacker to his knees with the power of his blows. Floundering in the mud the Norman did not even see the killer strike when it arrived, and Waltheof watched in admiration as the follow-up severed his head to send it spinning away. Despite the intensity of the attack, the earl's expression lit up as the housecarl shot him a wink on his return to the line, and they began to move forward together as another Norman broke through. Brand swung overhead and the attacker moved his shield to parry;

but the move was a feint and Waltheof's sword blade was already punching through mail and woollen undershirt to bury itself in his belly before the man could react.

As the Norman fell away and Brand's sword chopped down to finish him off, Waltheof stole a look along the line. Several of the housecarls had been overwhelmed by the onslaught, and although the remainder were fighting manfully to close the gaps the earl knew that the time to retreat had arrived. He called back across his shoulder as he watched the next wave of Normans approach the cut. 'Hrafn?'

His banner man replied instantly. 'Yes, lord?'

'Make the signal to withdraw.'

The war horn sang, its drawn-out pitch deepening as the sound trailed away. Immediately the shield wall contracted as the line bowed until the ends anchored themselves against the sides of the buildings flanking the roadway. Waltheof threw a look to the west and was thankful to see that Cospatric and his men had followed suit, backing up against the warren of alleyways which had carried them to the clearing. As the line opened up to readmit the surviving axemen, Waltheof was glad to see that Ulf of Torksey had heard the command and had finally abandoned his position on the bridge. Bespattered with the blood and gore of his foemen, the hulking axeman resembled a *dēofol* from Hell as he cut his way back towards safety, and Waltheof clasped the man by the sleeve as he regained the English line. 'Welcome home Horatius!' he exclaimed. 'Get yourself back to the gatehouse, you have done enough for today.' The acclamation was met by a blank look but now was not the time to describe the heroism of an ancient Roman, and the earl sent the man to the rear with a hefty clap on his slab-like shoulder.

With the attack on the burh apparently thwarted, the ferocity of the Norman assault lessened as the English retreated back down the roadway behind a wall of shields. They may have been rebuffed but their fighting qualities were undiminished, and no man would want to throw his life away needlessly against a strong defence flanked by walls of flame. Within a short time the first men were back in the courtyard before the gatehouse, and Waltheof thrilled to the sight as he ran his eyes along the burh walls. The wooden paling and walkways were sheets of flame, and lowering his gaze the earl saw that the twin doors had been wrenched from their posts and carried away. Soon the fire would spread to engulf the gateway itself — it was time to leave. 'Out you go lads,' he called as the final fighters seeped into the clearing, 'we have done all we set out to do.'

As the last men leapt into the saddle and cantered away, Norman spears finally appeared on the road; Waltheof backed through an arc of flame, Brand, Cospatric and Swegn at his side, and slinging their shields upon their backs to guard against a last ditch spear or arrow strike they remounted and put back their heels. Once out of bowshot the little group drew rein, twisting in the saddle to look back at their handiwork. Directly ahead the first hint of dawn was breaking beyond Wallingford, the burning town creating a corona of light against a wish-wash sky. Waltheof looked across to the West hoping to gauge the success of the attack, but darkness still reigned there.

Cospatric hawked and spat as the first Normans appeared illuminated by the flames. 'Do you think Wæcnan was successful?'

The earl shrugged. 'We gave him every chance, kinsman. Let us break our fast and see.'

'Ay up, here he comes — William the conqueror!'

Hoots of laughter came from the horsemen on the hill, and they watched the slow procession with unconcealed glee as the Normans crossed the bridge from the town and began to ascend the slope. Beyond the leading men the flags of Northumbria, Mercia and Wessex snapped taut in a freshening wind; above them dirty white clouds pregnant with the first snows of winter scurried away to the Northeast. Three days had passed since Ulfketil Wæcnan and his band of rustlers had chased away all but a handful of the Norman mounts, days in which the combined armies of the English folk had watched the trapped invaders frantically throwing up makeshift walls over the charred remains of Waltheof's attack. They need not have hurried. Trapped far from the sea and with the great metropolis of London guarding the lower Thames they were beyond succour and going nowhere.

Oswulf Eadwulfson spoke again, the Bernician's rough humour setting laughter ringing across the hillside once more. 'I don't know about you lads, but I always imagined him to be taller.'

The Norman leaders were almost up with them now, the fear and uncertainty about their own futures etched upon their features. Morcar edged his horse forward as the delegation drew to a halt, and Waltheof shared a fleeting look with his cousin and the Bernician at the presumption. His apparent leadership had been self-imposed, and although his brother Edwin showed his support, it was clear from the faces surrounding them that he was alone. Both men were Mercians, and the men of the North had not fought long and hard to throw off the yoke of southern rule only to have it reimposed at the moment of victory.

Morcar stole a glance at the trophy they had all come to see, before indicating that Stigand join him by the raising of a hand. 'Your Grace,' he said as the Normans stood in mute discomfort. 'You alone have met the duke. Would you do us all the kindness of confirming that we have our man?'

The archbishop of Canterbury left King Edgar of Wessex's side and walked his mount across. One glance was enough, and the old churchman gave a nod. Morcar spoke again. 'Lift it high,' he ordered, 'and show it to the men.'

As the shamefaced Normans raised the head, Waltheof gazed upon the unseeing eyes of the dead. He felt no pity, the duke had brought it upon himself by his avarice; William had been tricked into his invasion by the promises of his kinsman the Confessor. Waltheof snorted as the poll of the duke was paraded before the victors and the ground shook with their cries and chants. How the old man had hidden his hatred of Godwin and his clan for so long was impressive, conniving with young Edgar and the old lords of Wessex even until the very moment of his death to rid them of the Godwinson upstarts. But the men of the North needed no lessons in feuding, and his face took on the mien of the wolf as he looked back at the Mercian earl of the Northumbrians. The man thought that he was returning to York to be crowned king, but he would be disappointed. He snorted again. The matter was already in hand — he was riding to his death.

AFTERWORD

The genesis of *Wallingford Burh* came from a remark, which I have italicised below, contained within the only contemporary English account of the Battle of Hastings to have come down to us today, found in the Worcester manuscript of the Anglo-Saxon Chronicle. The final line of the entry for 1066 — 'When God wills, may the end be good' — the reference to William as king, and of course the fact that it was an ongoing annal of events within the kingdom, support the view that the passage was very likely written at the end of that tumultuous year, and as such it bears repeating here:

> Then King William came from Normandy into Pevensey, on the eve of the Feast of St. Michael, and as soon as they were fit, made a castle at Hastings market-town. Then this became known to King Harold and he gathered a great raiding-army, and came against him at the grey apple-tree. And William came upon him by surprise before his people were marshalled. Nevertheless the king fought very hard against him *with those men who wanted to support him*, and there was a great slaughter on either side. There were killed

> King Harold, and Earl Leofwine his brother, and Earl Gyrth his brother, and many good men. And the French had possession of the place of slaughter, just as God granted them because of the people's sins.

In the preceding tales I have taken the traditional view that England was united behind its king, but what if that is the perspective we ourselves have inherited as a result of Victorian romanticism in the nineteenth century, when the events of 1066 and King Harold's plucky army first gained widespread popularity? If we look again at the origins of those men known to have fought at Hastings listed at the end of *Hacon,* we can see that they all came from south-east of a line drawn from the Wash to the Isle of Wight, in other words the earldoms of king Harold and his brothers Gyrth and Leofwine. This may well reflect the levy system operating in England at that time and the losses already incurred during the fighting against Hardrada in the north, but the fact that Abbott Leofric of Peterborough was said to have fallen ill during the march to Hastings and left Harold's army would seem innocent enough until it is realised that he was a cousin of Edwin and Morcar.

Despite the fact that the earls of Mercia and Northumbria were referred to by Orderic Vitalis — who was born in England in 1075 and is viewed as a reliable source by historians — as 'Harold's close friends and adherents,' Edwin and Morcar were in fact the sons of Godwin's great rival Alfgar of Mercia. Alfgar actually gained the earldom of East Anglia for a short time from Harold Godwinson during the family's exile in 1051/52 so they were dynastic adversaries. Even if the sons of Godwin and Alfgar had patched up their differences, there must have been plenty of others within England at that time who felt aggrieved at what historian Michael

Wood described as a family of *nouveaux riches* controlling the kingdom. Godwin had risen from the thegnly class, and elites of any age seldom stand aside while their wealth and power are usurped by the lower orders, so it would be unsurprising if the leading families of Wessex would long for a return of the old order represented by Edgar ætheling.

This feeling must have been even stronger in the North. Waltheof, the hero of our tale, was the younger son of Siward Digri (Siward the Strong), the earl of Northumbria who had died in 1055. With the death of his elder brother in battle the previous year and too young to inherit his father's title, the earldom had gone to Tostig Godwinson whose misrule had ended in open rebellion as already described in another of our tales, *Peace Weaver*. Waltheof is the only earl not mentioned in the fighting of 1066, and as Harold Godwinson's route north to fight Hardrada passed through his lands we must assume that he fought there. He submitted to William following the defeat at Hastings and was confirmed in his earldom, but after continuous involvement in various blood feuds and uprisings, most notably the Revolt of the Earls in 1075, he managed to accrue to himself an unenviable claim to fame when he became the only Anglo-Saxon noble executed on king William's orders.

Certainly the families of the leading men in the North, men like Oswulf Eadwulfson of Bamburgh and Waltheof's cousin Cospatric, had seen invaders come and go for centuries without losing their hold on power. Only Harold Godwinson among the English leaders in 1066 had recent experience of continental warfare: only he had seen the way in which land was taken and held by a system of castles and mounted knights, and it was the probable reason why he chose to move quickly against William's invasion force before they could advance inland. That the northerners thought they could survive, and even reach a kind of power-sharing arrangement similar to the old Danelaw is reflected in their actions following Harold's defeat at Hastings; but they were to be cruelly disappointed, the various uprisings and revolts only inviting the retaliation known as the Harrying of the North in the winter of 1069/70.

If there had been any degree of unity within the English nation following the defeat at Hastings, William's crowning that year would have been unlikely. The Norman army was reduced first by losses in battle, and then the onset of dysentery while encamped at Dover. After a strong detachment of knights was repulsed when it reached London, the duke did undertake what in later centuries would have been known as a *chevauchée,* a destructive march through enemy territory, which skirted the city, captured Winchester, and crossed the River Thames at its lowest fordable place at Wallingford. In reality the fractured English opposition made its first submission here in the form of Stigand archbishop of Canterbury, as the Normans built a castle at the Northeast corner of the burh. A few weeks later William and his army were in Berkhamstead north of London where the remaining English leaders submitted, and on Christmas Day 1066, after a march which had covered more than 350 miles, William was crowned king at Westminster Abbey and the Anglo-Saxon age came to an end.

A BONUS TALE

11

THE YEAR OF THE RAVEN

Tytherley - Hampshire

Midsummer 1016

Hereswith paused at the threshold and cocked her head, concentrating hard as she shifted the weight of the bundle in her arms. All that carried to her were the muted sounds of summer: crickets rasping in the meadow; the cooing of a dove in the copse above the hall. Shaking her head, she chastised herself as she ducked inside and crossed to feed the hearth.

You are imagining things now, you foolish woman!

Setting the load down she picked out a stalk, poking about in the ash before adding more fuel as the logs settled in a flurry of embers. Flames showed as the bark caught, and satisfied with her efforts Hereswith straightened up and gave the pottage a stir. The vegetable content was diminishing by the day, soon they would be living on little more than a watery soup. High summer was the hardest season of all, a time when folk were scraping the barrel for the last of the previous year's harvest as they prayed for the new. During the worst years it was common to find the old and the poor so weak that they could barely stand, and more than a few resorted to selling their children into slavery to ensure they survived at all. And now the Danes had returned.

Lost in her thoughts she failed to hear the approaching footfalls until a shadow fell across the floor, and she glanced up as the silhouette of her daughter filled the doorway. 'Did you not hear it, mother?'

Hereswith was instantly alert. 'I thought I was dreaming it. What did you hear girl?'

Edith beckoned her mother outside as the sound grew louder: 'a horse.'

THE GROUP of riders shared a smile and urged their mounts down from the crest of the hill: another undefended farmstead. Was it any wonder that their kings and jarls had returned to the kingdoms in the West time after time, before the days of their grandfathers even?

At the foot of the slope a woman came from the building, reaching out to take her daughter's hand as the four riders approached.

Starkad threw his friends a grin. 'Is she going to run, boys? I say yes, the winner goes first: Skuli?'

The Dane craned forward in the saddle and studied their intended victim. After a short pause he shook his head slowly. 'She'll not run.'

Starkad's face lit up. 'We have a contest! Otkel?'

Otkel shrugged. 'She looks a bit scrawny for me, but I will play.' He sucked at his teeth as he studied the woman's posture. He prided himself as a swordsman and he had learned long ago how to read the moment when an enemy decided to fight or flee. 'No,' he said finally. 'She will stay put.'

Starkad beamed and looked across the line of riders to the man on the far side. 'It looks as though it's between us then, Einar. Are you in this time or not?'

The big Dane shook his head. 'The only part of me that needs feeding is my stomach. I will root around and see what I can find until you can spare the time to help.' He cast a flinty look towards the leader of the party. 'That is why we were sent out, unless our orders have changed?'

Otkel reached across and clapped him on the shoulder. 'That must be some woman you have at home.' He shot his friends a sly wink. 'I promise to go and break the sad news to her when the English catch you one day.'

A chorus of laughter rose into the midsummer air, and Einar was about to reply but thought better of it. He was new to the group — not yet fully accepted. If they could not control their urges that was their problem.

Starkad slapped the neck of his mount in delight. 'It looks as though I get to go first again after all.'

Skuli turned on him. 'Why should you go first? She still hasn't moved, and you said that she would be a runner.'

Starkad threw them a nonchalant shrug. 'Einar is not playing and you two agree. You can't both go first, so it looks as if it will have to be me. Besides,' he continued with a sneer, 'I am the leader of our little band. You two will have to take your turn.'

As the others argued over the woman Einar remained watchful, his eyes scanning the valley as he looked for any signs that men were about. For all the fools knew the barn ahead of them contained a dozen armed rustics, or even the local thegn and his men. If that *was* the case they were probably already dead. Not for the first time that day he cursed the man whose sickness had caused him to become attached to Starkad's ragged band of cutthroats.

Einar raised his eyes as the quartet clicked the mounts on, searching the furthest slopes of the valley as they came up to the outbuildings. If he was going to be the only one in the open, it was as well that he ensured that the tree line was not about to disgorge the men of the local fyrd. Even country boys armed with scythes and sickles could be dangerous to a man whose trews were around his ankles. The twin figures seemed transfixed by the sudden appearance of four horsemen in the valley, and Einar felt the familiar sinking feeling in his guts as they fanned out and dropped down the bank into the yard which stood before the hall.

Slipping from the saddle the Danes drew their swords with a flourish, sweeping them in a circle as they asked the usual question. *'Menn?'*

The woman cast her eyes to the ground and shook her head sadly. No, there were no men to come to her aid. Starkad grunted with satisfaction. If there had been he would have had to kill them, and it always seemed to spoil the moment. Sheathing his sword he indicated a rickety enclosure which in happier times must have held the family horse. The English woman's gaze flicked from her daughter to the corral and back to the Danish leader, and Einar watched in admiration as she cleared her throat and glared: 'just me.'

Starkad looked the girl over and seemed to be considering taking them both. The girl was pretty; hair the colour of damp hay was gathered together by a strip of blue linen. The summer sun had blushed her cheeks and nose, and Einar knew that it was only the fact that the girl was barely six winters old that would save her. Even Starkad appeared to set some limits to his debauchery, but even so he tapped out a beat on the hilt of his sword as he fixed his part-time leader with a stare. Starkad's eyes widened in surprise as he recognised the implied threat, but although he snorted in derision the hostility in his eyes revealed his true feelings, and Einar knew that he would have to watch his back for the remainder of the time he was with the army of Cnut. Starkad reached out to tousle the girl's hair as he and Einar held each other's gaze, but he finally nodded his agreement to the woman's request, and Einar watched as her shoulders sagged with a mixture of relief and dread.

The English woman turned to her daughter and raised the girl's chin until their eyes met; holding her gaze she stroked her hair and spoke in the tone which Einar recalled his wife use with their own children. It was the voice of a woman who would brook no argument and it was instantly recognisable to any parent or child, regardless of the language used. 'Go inside and remain there until I come to you.' The mother leaned forward and kissed the child lightly on the forehead before they locked eyes once again. 'Do you understand me?' The girl nodded sadly as her mother attempted to introduce a note of cheeriness into her final words. 'Off you go then.'

As the young girl disappeared into the shadowy interior, Einar took up his spear and began to cross to the small barn. Taking a backwards glance he was just in time to see the woman bend forward across the fencing, the full moon of her buttocks stark in the sunlight as the Danish leader made a bundle of her kirtle and tossed it onto her back.

EDITH TURNED BACK and shaded her eyes against the glare as she searched out the source of the oncoming hoofbeats. Her mother crossed from the hearth and ducked back into the sunlight. 'What can you see?'

The girl shook her head and chewed her lower lip in alarm. 'It's not coming from the lane,' she said finally. 'It sounds like it is coming from the rear of the hall.'

Mother and daughter shared a look of unease. Nobody came across the fields unless they were unfamiliar with the local roads or there was trouble in the Hundred. Either way, both of them quickly realised that the day which they knew could come at any time had finally arrived. Instinctively, Hereswith slipped her hand into her daughter's as they rounded the angle of the hall and walked to the rear. Edith was the first to clear the woodpile, and the girl let out a squeal as the rider hove into view. 'It's Aldwulf!'

Hereswith closed her eyes and sighed with relief. Ever since the Danes had returned to their lands, the people of Wessex had lived with the ever present fear that a war band would suddenly appear in their parish. The king had called out the fyrd earlier that summer as the enemy had swept through the lands of the Mercians to the north of the Thames, and men were still thin on the ground. Since king Alfred's time the free men of fighting age had been divided into thirds. In times of war one-third went to the king's army and one-third to guard the nearest fortified town, the local burh. That left barely enough able bodied men of the Hundred to manage the everyday life of the community.

Hereswith forced herself to remain calm as Aldwulf cantered down the slope towards them. Despite her daughter's joy at seeing the young noble, the boy's expression told her that all was not well. She patted Edith on the shoulder. 'Go and fetch ale for Aldwulf. He looks as though he has ridden hard.'

Delighted with her task Edith scampered away, and her

mother turned her attention back to the young rider as he began to slow his mount. The boy was the same age, ten winters, and she had begun to plant the idea in people's minds that the pair were a good match. Her husband was a stalwart of the village and a fierce warrior, well regarded in all the right halls. Only that spring Cutha had been appointed *cumbolwiga* to Aldwulf's father Aldhelm, the thegn's standard-bearer in battle; it was a high honour, and Hereswith was determined that it was one which would be used to advance the fortunes of her family. She painted her face with a welcoming smile as the object of her scheming clattered into the yard.

'There are Danes in the Hundred!'

Hereswith reached up and grasped the bridle, calming the horse with a stroke of its muzzle as she quizzed the boy. 'Where were they last seen, Aldwulf?'

Before he could reply Edith reappeared, offering up the cup of ale with a coyness she had taught the girl for this very moment, before curling a finger to hook away a strand of hair left deliberately loose. Despite the seriousness of the boy's errand, it was all Hereswith could do not to hug the girl as she followed up with a saucy smile.

Naturally Aldwulf gave no indication that he had noticed any of it, but Hereswith knew that the hunted were often the last to realise the fact until it was too late for them.

The boy took the drink with a nod of thanks and drained it in one. 'Cnut's army is still well to the north of Wallop,' he blurted out. 'But they have parties of horsemen foraging all over.' He made a fist and pushed it into his stomach, belching softly as the ale repeated on him.

'Cutha has our horse,' she replied. 'We will never reach Salisbury burh before we are overtaken.' Hereswith's gaze wandered across the hillside as her mind worked on the options available to her. 'Carry on and warn the other farmsteads,' she said finally, 'my husband has built us a hiding place nearby.' Aldwulf nodded, pulling on the reins as he guided his mount towards the far field. Hereswith called after him as he exited the yard. 'Aldwulf, take care. If you are overtaken don't act rashly and get yourself killed; give them what they want and let them go on their way. Your day will come.'

The boy pulled a pained expression, and Hereswith could not help but chuckle at his reply. 'You are the fifth woman to tell me that this morning, not including my mother and sisters.' He snorted as the horse moved into a canter. 'Even a skull as thick as mine cannot ignore the soundness of the advice!'

They parted with a wave, and Hereswith began to collect her thoughts as Aldwulf made the lane. He had better be careful she mused as she watched him go, he was the best catch for miles around. She turned back as her daughter retrieved the cup. 'Edith, you know what to do. We can't take the last of the grain from the store, but they are not getting the hog if they come here. Fetch the box containing our silver from the eaves while I grab Crackling, and we will get up to the wood.'

THE DANES SHARED a look as the sound of a horse carried to them from the clearing ahead. They had been watering their mounts at the small brook in the shade of a tree lined bank, and the experienced scouts instinctively moved to take up positions athwart the road, hefting their shields, couching their spears as they waited for the rider to appear around the bend. Within moments the horse hove into view, and the tension left their faces as the rider was revealed to be not much more than a boy.

Aldwulf gasped in horror as he entered the woodland and came face to face with a line of heavily armed raiders. For a heartbeat he considered urging his horse forward in an attempt to burst through the wall which had sprung up barring his path, but the women's advice came back to him and he hauled at the reins and tried to remain calm.

Starkad clicked his tongue, and his horse walked forward as the others ranged to either side. 'Nice horse.'

Aldwulf rested his hands on the saddle horn, staring straight ahead lest his eyes betray the hatred he felt for the invaders.

Starkad reached across, removing the boy's sword from its scabbard and examined it with a smirk: 'nice sword, too!' He threw a look across his shoulder and spoke to the others. 'It looks as though we have caught ourselves a jarl, lads!' He pulled a mocking smile as Aldwulf finally met his gaze. 'Are you a jarl, boy?'

The young West Saxon composed himself and answered with barely concealed contempt. 'It would seem not as you still live. If I were a jarl, would not the men of my *lith* have cut you down by now?'

Starkad's eyes widened in surprise. 'Your *lith* eh? A good Danish name. You seem to know a lot about us lad, maybe you can even read? Perhaps we should take you along with us for ransom: how much do you think your family would pay?'

Einar edged his mount forward as the others hung back. 'Let the boy go Starkad, we don't have the time for this. The army needs food not another mouth to feed. Empty his purse, take his horse and send him on his way. We need to keep moving.'

Starkad glowered at his countryman, before raising his

spear to tap the leaf shaped blade against Aldwulf's cheek. The boy stiffened but kept his eyes fixed on his tormentor. 'What do you say boy? Is my tender-hearted friend right? Should I let you go?'

Aldwulf hesitated before he replied. Despite all the womanly advice he had received that morning his temper was rising at the Dane's impudence — he was the son of a thegn, if his life was to end here he would die like one. Already annoyed by Einar's challenge the look of defiance was all the excuse the Dane needed, and the spear blade stabbed forward to winkle the boy from the saddle. As Aldwulf hit the ground with a gasp of shock and pain, Einar started at the suddenness of the violence. 'Why?' he gasped as he began to recover his wits. 'He was no danger, he could not have got very far on foot!'

Starkad rounded on him as the others averted their eyes. 'Listen you fool. I don't know what kind of war you have been fighting before today, but even you must have noticed that innocent people get killed. If you don't want to plough their women that's your loss, but what do you think this poor mite has been up to this morning?' Starkad edged his mount across with a squeeze of his knees, spitting the following words through gritted teeth. 'Do you think he was out for a nice ride in the sunshine? Or perhaps he was calling on a girl? What do you think? It *is* a lovely day.' The big Dane pulled a face as though an idea had just occurred to him. 'Or maybe he has been riding all over the area? Warning people that there are Danes about?' He clicked his fingers as the others began to shift uneasily in their saddles. They had seen this mood before and it usually ended in more bloodshed than a simple shoulder wound. 'Yes, that's it!' he exclaimed. 'It all makes sense now. The fine horse: the sword; rushing about like a fool straight into a party of heathen killers.' He encompassed the group with a sweep of his spear as Aldwulf watched nervously from the leaf litter beneath them. 'The heathen killers bit, that's us, remember that. Now, let's get going before the men that our friend here will have alerted come in force against us.'

Otkel cut in as he saw Einar was about to make a reply. He could see that Starkad's anger was about to boil over and he knew from experience that it invariably ended in a death. They were still deep within enemy territory and they needed to keep their wits about them if they were not to end up as grisly entertainment for the locals. He had seen the bodies of men who had been taken before and he had no wish to join them. The women were the worst, and his hand moved instinctively to his groin; all it would take is one word out of place from the new boy and anything could happen. 'Starkad is right, Einar,' he said. 'There could be armed men gathering against us even as we sit here. One more farm and I say we return to Cnut — use the boy's mount as a pack horse and go.' He glanced down at Aldwulf and sniffed. 'It's your lucky day, boy. Take yourself off home and get the wound dressed. You will have a nice scar to show the girls — when the tale has grown to how you faced down fifty savage Danes all alone, and lived to tell the tale.'

Flipping the wattle panel aside, Hereswith peered inside despite the urgency she felt. The last time they had used the shelter it had been full of creepy crawlies, and she was not about to jump blindly in and land on heaven-knows what. Old Ælfheah in the next valley had climbed into his Dane hole and found himself sharing it with a half starved fox which had fallen in and couldn't climb back out. It was only the fact that his knife had been to hand which had saved him from the crazed animal.

Satisfied that the hole was clean and safe, she lowered herself in and held out a hand for the leash. Edith tossed the rope across, before dropping to her knees to shoulder the protesting swine to the lip of the pit as her mother gave a tug. As the hog toppled into the hole with a squeal, Hereswith held up her arms. 'Come on then, in you come.' As Edith backed over the edge, Hereswith guided her foot into the notch cut into the side wall which acted as a step. 'Make a good job with the leaves, there's a good girl.'

Edith scooped an armful of dead leaves from the forest floor and spread them thickly across the upper surface of the wattle before sliding it into place it with her fingertips. As the girl jumped down and made a fuss of the pig, Hereswith craned her neck and searched the wattle screen for a chink of light. Satisfied that it was completely covered, she lifted the edge of the panel a sliver and propped it open with a small stick.

They had reached safety with moments to spare. Four horsemen were coming into the yard, and mindful of the girl beneath her in the dark she had stifled a cry of anguish. Despite the fact that it was laden down with plunder, Hereswith had recognised the horse they led as the one which had carried young Aldwulf away only a short while before. Closing her eyes she sent a prayer to God that they had only robbed the boy and sent him on his way.

Her hideaway was well constructed and perfectly placed, overlooking the farm and its surroundings. Most outlying farms and halls had such bolt holes for use when invaders or wolf heads were in the area, but few were as good as the one which Cutha had built for them. Lined with stout oak planking, the floor had been raised above the earth on joists helping to keep the damp at bay. Positioned to give the occupants an uninterrupted view down the valley, Hereswith watched as the Danes dismounted and began to search.

'Look at this boys, it is our lucky day!' Skuli beamed as he slurped the soup from the big wooden spoon; 'lovely.'

Delighted grins came to the faces of the raiders as they saw that a hot meal was in the offing. Starkad placed a palm on Einar's chest as he went to follow Otkel into the hall. 'Not you, someone needs to stay on guard. Broth doesn't make itself and it could be a trap. You were keen on finding more grain before, now is your chance.' He threw him a mocking smile. 'We'll save you some.'

Einar fought back the retort which came to him. It was obvious that he had been chosen because of his challenge at the burn, and he realised that the man was waiting to see how he would respond. If he rose to the bait the situation could quickly become heated, even fatal for one of the pair, and both men knew that they were far from help. If an English war band did turn up unexpectedly and they were fighting among themselves or stuffing their faces inside it would not go well for them. He forced a smile to his face and nodded as he turned away.

As the eager yapping of hungry men around a cooking pot filled the air, the Dane ran his eyes over the neat and ordered farmyard. It was so like his own back in Jutland, and he felt a pang of homesickness at the sight. He would be there still if the scrapie had not taken practically his entire flock, and he longed for the time when he had stolen enough silver from the people here to head home and replace his ravaged stock. A small enclosure caught his eye, and the Dane sauntered across to take a peek over the waist high fence. A sty nestled at the far end of the dusty enclosure and Einar slapped his thigh with delight as he squatted down to peer inside, but although he was already salivating at the thought of the meal to come he saw to his disappointment that the interior was empty.

A brace of wood pigeons clattered into the air and he swung about in alarm, spear held at the ready as his minds-eye imagined the woodland spewing forth the local thegn and his war band. Relieved when nothing more threatening emerged he lifted his chin, tracing the flight of the birds as they beat their way aloft before gliding across the clearing towards a small copse. The wooded knoll was clearly managed, and Einar felt himself drawn towards the stand of poker-straight trees. Even at a distance he could see that the open spaces between the coppiced saplings were ankle deep in leaf mould. It was the perfect place for hogs to root for mast, and Einar smiled to himself as he started up the small slope. Perhaps he would get to taste swine flesh today after all.

DESPITE THE DISTANCE BETWEEN THEM, Hereswith instinctively drew her head away from the opening and mewed in fear. The Dane was marching straight up the hill, his eyes turning directly towards the hiding place, and she allowed the wattle to fall back into place as she dropped to the floor. She hissed at Edith as she reached across and took the piglet from her. 'There is a Dane coming this way. Keep quiet and still and he will pass us by.'

The girl shrank back into the corner and Hereswith seized the unfortunate piglet by the snout and yanked its head back. One quick draw of the knife across its throat was enough to open both jugular and she hugged the animal into her, smothering its dying kicks and stifling the last terrified squeals. 'Sorry Crackling, but we can't have you giving us away.' Hereswith held on until the animal had stilled and dropped it to the floor. She looked across to her daughter and pulled a sad smile. Even in the darkness of the Dane hole she looked shocked at the sudden violence of the piglet's death, and although the girl knew what the fate of every animal on the farm would be, she *had* been fond of him.

CRIES AND LAUGHTER carried up to Einar as he laboured up the slope, and he shook his head in dismay. Starkad and his cronies had a death wish and he was glad to be away from them. If they made it back to the army in one piece, he would ensure that he was far away when men were being assigned to foraging parties in the future. He leaned in to his spear as the hillside steepened. The edge of the copse was just ahead, and he began to run his eyes across the woodland floor as he searched for signs of disturbance. Swine were notorious for the mess they made and any signs should be easy to spot.

The tiniest of movements off to the left caught his eye and his head spun around as he brought his spear to bear. Einar froze as he waited for the movement to repeat itself but all remained still. Hogs were intelligent creatures and they knew full well what a spear was used for — if he was gored out here it would be the end of him. He had no doubt that Starkad and the others would abandon him to the locals, and he was under no illusions as to his fate if that did happen.

Placing his feet deliberately, he edged between the nearest spray of saplings and moved into the trees. The sun was overhead and the light was streaming down through the leafy canopy, illuminating every dip and mound of the woodland floor, and he gripped his spear tightly as the bright light picked out the distinctive weave of wattle just ahead. Einar jumped aside as he realised what he had discovered, throwing himself behind the bole of a tree as he imagined an arrow trained on him from the hideaway. His mind raced. He dare not turn away and call to the others — even a single moment of inattention here could cost him his life. Besides, the sounds coming from the hall told him that they had discovered the ale supplies and he doubted that they would care. It was likely that the pit before him contained only women, children and men too old to fight, and he could imagine what would happen if the others did come up. Einar edged his head around the tree trunk, fixing his gaze upon the wattle screen as he spoke. 'Slide back the cover, and place your hands on the lip of the hole where I can see them. Do it quickly and no harm will come to you.'

The Dane waited expectantly, but neither movement or any sound followed his instruction. Despite the potential danger, he found that he was smiling at the absurdity of the situation. If there was nobody actually in there, he was hiding behind a tree in a foreign copse talking to an empty hole in the ground. He was about to move forward to edge the wattle aside with the tip of his spear when several fingertips spidered their way into view and inched back the panel.

Einar tensed and hefted his spear. If armed men did spring from the ground he would have to use the spear as a javelin and draw his sword quickly. He wished now that he had thought to bring his shield along but it was still tied to the flank of his horse. He cleared his throat, trying to sound as confident as possible as he gestured to imaginary companions with his spear. 'All of you, place your hands where we can see them.'

A single pair of hands gripped the lip of the hiding place

and a voice tainted by fear called out. 'There are only two of us, and my daughter cannot reach.'

Einar's head moved from side to side as his eyes stabbed the shadows, suspecting a trap, but finally satisfied that they were alone he spoke again to the anxious sounding woman. 'Are you armed?'

A knife was tossed from the hole in response, and the Dane took a backwards step as he saw the blade was streaked with blood. Raising his eyes he noticed for the first time that the woman's hands were also sticky with it, and he tensed again as his worries returned in a flash. Einar held the point of the spear towards the dark square on the woodland floor as he crept cautiously towards the lip. 'Whose blood is on your hands?'

To his surprise the answer carried up from the depths of the hole, and the Viking recognised that the tearful voice belonged to a young girl. 'Crackling's — it is Crackling's blood.'

The girl's mother cut in quickly to clear up any confusion; the situation was dangerous enough without the Dane thinking they were killers. 'Crackling was our swine. I killed him because he was too noisy and might give us away.'

Einar snorted as his mind slowly teased apart the weft and weave of the dialect. He understood the English used in the eastern parts of the country, the regions of the old Danelaw of East Anglia, the Midlands and York with ease and could speak it of a fashion. It was not, after all, so different from his own tongue. The words used in the Saxon lands south of the River Thames were more difficult, more like those used by their cousins in Saxony and Frisia; but they were familiar enough to a well-travelled man such as himself, and he shook his head and pulled a wry smile at the girl's revelation. 'You called your swine Crackling?' He stole a quick look inside the hole and saw the girl cradling Crackling's bloodstained body, pulling a face at the sorry sight which met his eyes. 'I am sad for Crackling. To die in a hole is not the best of deaths.'

Einar's lament was interrupted as a roar of laughter rolled up the hill, and a loud crash carried from the hall causing the Dane to flush with embarrassment. The sound had reminded him of the men who awaited them in the valley below, and he looked again at the pair through new eyes. The mother was a fine looking woman, plump in the right places with plaits of chestnut brown hair framing a comely face. Her daughter shared her features and was definitely old enough to interest Starkad, especially now that he had discovered the ale store. He indicated that the woman lower her hands from the lip of the den as he asked a question. 'There are no men hereabouts?' He could understand the fear he saw in the woman's eyes, but he needed to be sure for his own safety and he tried again. 'You must answer me truthfully if I am to help you. I give you my word that I will not harm either of you.'

The woman hesitated a moment longer as she weighed up her captor. Finally she came to the decision that trustworthy or not, she would have to take a chance. She shook her head. 'No, my man is away.' She paused again, fixing Einar with a stare as a note of defiance entered her voice. 'There are Vikings in our land,' she said, 'and he is carrying spear and shield against them.'

He nodded that he understood. 'I hope that he returns safely to you. These are not such good times.' He cast a look back down the hill. 'You are fortunate that I found you, if it had been one of the others....' He shrugged as his voice trailed away. 'Things would not have gone so well for you.'

Einar indicated that Hereswith duck back inside the refuge with a nod of his head. As he pulled the panel back across, the last the pair saw of him was the white of his smile.

'Stay here, we will be moving off soon.' He chuckled and spoke to nobody in particular as he began to back away. 'I can feast on swine flesh another day.'

The Dane kicked a thick covering of leaves across until he was certain that they were well hidden; shouldering the spear he began to retrace his steps down the hillside. As the slope bottomed out and he regained the courtyard, he reflected on the people he had met here in Wessex during the course of Cnut's invasion. He had just about amassed enough silver now to replace his stock, and he had no need to steal from other people, hard working families who looked and acted like his own. There were always men coming and going from the army, he would join one such band; make his way to the coast and take a ship for home as soon as they returned.

Einar filled his lungs as he walked. It was a fine day to be alive, and the good deed had raised his spirits after what had gone before. The sun was hot, and the English countryside lush with greenery. High above two ravens twisted and soared, tumbling earthwards in a ritual display, and he reached inside his shirt to finger the silver hammer of Thor which hung there. It had been a parting gift to him from Hild and Svein, his daughter and son back in Jutland, and the sight of Oðinn's birds brought a smile to his face as it prompted an image of them waving their goodbyes in his mind.

Einar settled on the wall of Crackling's old sty as he watched the antics of the dusky birds. The men back in camp were already calling this The Year of the Raven as the armies of Cnut and Erik of Hlathir rampaged across the English countryside, but they were acting curiously, weaving patterns in the summer sky, and he called out to them as he thought how his wife would attempt to interpret the movements as a message from the All-father himself. 'You have missed him

Huginn and Muninn,' he said with a smile. 'Young Crackling is already halfway across the rainbow bridge to Asgard.'

The smile slowly faded as his thoughts turned once again to home, but the flash of sunlight on polished steel drew his attention back to the roadway and the Dane's heart sank as he realised that the birds had not come for the swine after all. As the boy with the bloodied shoulder led the fyrdmen into the yard, Einar tucked the silver pendant back inside his shirt as he rose and drew his sword.

AFTERWORD

Although set fifty years before the Norman conquest, the inspiration for *The Year of the Raven* is a famous scene on the Bayeux Tapestry. A woman, one of only three depicted in the entire work along with Edward the Confessor's wife Eadgyth and a mysterious woman known only as Ælfgyfa, flees her home clutching the hand of her young son as invading soldiers touch brands to the roof thatch.

Almost 230 feet in length, the size of three Olympic pools laid end to end, the tapestry (actually an embroidery) is generally accepted to have been stitched by English women in Canterbury very soon after the events they portray. Canterbury is less than fifty miles from the scene of fighting that October day and paid host to the victorious invaders a few weeks later, so I like to think that this particular episode was slipped into the narrative as a cry for recognition amid the yards of space taken up by their menfolk. *Look here we are, your women and children. We suffered too!* It is a part of warfare still overlooked to this day. We watch as tanks and troops advance past burning buildings with barely a thought for the inhabitants, people who will now have to fight their own desperate war against hunger and the elements as they attempt to survive the snowy steppes of Russia or the sun baked fields of the Middle East.

But armies, even early medieval ones, are not filled with unthinking automata however much their leaders may wish them to be, and I was keen to add a touch of humanity to one such raider at least. Sickened by the whole thing, Einar recognises the inhabitants of the villages and farms of England as indistinguishable from the family he left behind in Denmark and is keen to return; that fate decreed otherwise is another small tragedy, as a boy and girl grow up fatherless not even knowing where or how he died. It's a vignette which must have played out in almost every campaign ever waged in every corner of the globe.

The Danish invasions which led to the conquest of Anglo-Saxon England in 1016 and the reign of Cnut the Great are the seed pod from which the later Norman takeover grew. The various characters and the parts they played during this sweep of history: Sweyn Forkbeard and his son Cnut; Queen Emma; Godwin and his Godwinsons; William of Normandy; Hardrada of Norway and the many others we have met in the preceding tales are well known to us, and I hope that you had as much enjoyment reading my alternative timelines for them as I did researching and writing them. If anything they show just how easily, and in so many ways, what we all think of as the progression of history can dramatically change direction. There were many other drafts which missed the cut: William's father Robert the Magnificent never undertakes a pilgrimage to Jerusalem or returns safely to take up rule again; neither Æthelræd of England nor Cnut the Dane marry and have children by Emma of Normandy; Osbearn, the son and heir of Earl Siward of Northumbria, survives the defeat of Macbeth of Alba in battle in 1054 thereby depriving Tostig Godwinson of the earldom when his father dies the following year are just a few.

Spear Havoc is the first time I have written both a collection of short stories and alternative history, and the views expressed in the various Afterwords are naturally my own. You may disagree with a few of my conclusions there, but the truth in many cases is unknowable and they are, I think, all part of the fun with this type of storytelling.

If this is the first time you have read any of my work, perhaps you would be interested in my full length novels? My first series, Sword of Woden is an imagining of the early life of the great northern hero Beowulf, from childhood to the fight with the monster Grendel and a little beyond. The timeline continues with King's Bane which is set in the time of the Anglo-Saxon migrations to what is now England, while my Conqueror of Rome duo concern the Trans-Alpine migration of a Gaulish tribe under the war leader Brennus and the subsequent sack of Rome. My latest trilogy, Erik Haraldsson, tells the life story of the last king of an independent Northumbria, better known to history as Erik Bloodaxe. Details of all my books can be found at the end of this volume.

I am always grateful when readers recommend my books to others, it really does help independent authors such as myself gain visibility and recognition. I love to read reviews for my work on Amazon, Goodreads, social media or blogs, so if you can spare a few moments to write a line or two it is always appreciated. It is a vital source of feedback for me and you can help other readers at the same time. If you would like to contact me directly, please feel free to do so via the links at the bottom of the following 'About the Author' page. We all share a fondness for history, and I always enjoy the interaction.

Cliff May
East Anglia
September 2019

ABOUT THE AUTHOR

Cliff May is a writer of historical fiction, working primarily in the early Middle Ages. He has always had a love of history which led to an early career in conservation work. Using the knowledge and expertise gained he moved with his family through a succession of dilapidated houses which he single-handedly renovated. These ranged from a Victorian town-house to a Fourteenth Century hall, and he added childcare to his knowledge of medieval oak frame repair, wattle and daub and lime plastering. Cliff crewed the replica of Captain Cook's ship, Endeavour, sleeping in a hammock and sweating in the sails and travelled the world, visiting such historic sites as the Little Big Horn, Leif Eriksson's Icelandic birthplace and the bullet scarred walls of Berlin's Reichstag.

Now he writes, only a stone's throw from the Anglian ship burial site at Sutton Hoo in East Anglia.

cmay2808@yahoo.co.uk

ALSO BY C. R. MAY

TWELVE BROTHERS
ONE CROWN
C.R. MAY
BLOODAXE
ERIK HARALDSSON I

BLOODAXE

THE RAVEN AND THE CROSS

EVERY LEGEND HAS A BEGINNING
C.R. MAY
SORROW HILL
BEOWULF - SWORD OF WODEN I

SORROW HILL

WRÆCCA

MONSTERS

DAYRAVEN

FIRE AND STEEL

GODS OF WAR

THE SCATHING

TERROR GALLICUS

NEMESIS